A Matter of Grace
Nazi Germany to America
One Woman's Journey of Faith

A Matter of Grace

Nazi Germany to America
One Woman's Journey of Faith

Trudy Gronning

Raber Publishing
2018

First Printing: 2018
ISBN 978-1-387-40104-8

Photographs courtesy of the author's private collection except for pages 37 and 48 which are courtesy of Pixabay.

A Matter of Grace is dedicated to:
John
Larry & Judy
Tom, Michelle, Cade & Bryce
Jim, Lori, Amma, & Alana
Rick & Kelly
Kitty & Ransom
Hubert

To my family & friends who have all gone before me

My grandfather Hans Raab
Court purveyor to King Ludwig II

My loving parents
Hans Raab & Karolina Raab

My dear brothers
Hans Karl Michael Raab
Heinrich Wolfgang Julius Raab

My beloved childhood friends
Evi Gretz & Kurt Kaphan

Author Preface

The idea for this book first came to me in 1967 and with absolutely no skills as a writer I set off to create an autobiographical account of my life. I was earnest in my writing efforts, but I often allowed circumstances to put my words on hold so many times I lost count. Over the years I would get the familiar urge to put my thoughts on paper, make notes, and then put them all aside in a file that seemed to be marked "*Someday.*"

But, as I wrote my story, it was easier for me to share my experiences through fictional characters based on real people in my life. Thus, began an historical account of my journey as told through "Jane" who had become my voice.

Fifty years after I first put pencil to paper that great tug on my heart came again, the familiar urging to finish my story. The reminders came in many forms, from my restless conscience, from friends, but my age was the biggest motivator of all.

When I started writing I was just thirty-nine years old. As you hold my book in your hands, I have just celebrated my eighty-ninth birthday.

A Matter of Grace begins with my years growing up in Munich, Germany under Nazi rule, WWII and the horrors of war, and the persecution of Jews. It's about the challenges and changes I have endured these many decades, the absolute joy of coming to America, the heartbreak of watching my son march off to Vietnam, and the utter devastation of being diagnosed with MS, and a million other moments that tested my faith.

But I have also found God to be greater than all the challenges that came my way. As a child I learned "the evil of silence" and vowed to never again be silent in the face of cruelty and persecution. Today, I am witness to the persecution of Christians and Jews in my lifetime, something I thought I would never see again and that's the reason this book had to written.

Deepest thanks and gratitude to my friend and steadfast writing coach John St. Augustine, who helped me to finally bring my story to life. The file once marked as "*Someday*" is now labeled as "*Published.*"

Thank you for reading *A Matter of Grace.*

Trudy Gronning.

x

Prologue

The storm rolled in over the hills of Lancaster, Pennsylvania just before midnight. It was one of those slow rumbling mid-summer storms that had been gathering for some time. The hot July weather making it ripe for a collision with a cold front that would bring with it some relief to the cracked dry ground of Western Pennsylvania.

Lightning had been dancing across the walls in Jane Johnson's bedroom for nearly an hour before a formidable crack of thunder woke her from a sound sleep. The booming sound reminded her of another time many, many, years ago when she was a little girl. A quick glance to the bed on her right confirmed that her husband Chris was still asleep, at least for now. His years in the military had ingrained a deep sense of schedule, it was only 1:18 in the morning, and it would be several hours before his internal clock would wake him right on time at 5 a.m.

Unable to go back to sleep, she carefully pulled herself upright and swung her feet to the floor next to the walker that had become her constant companion in her later years. It was a steadying presence as she had gotten older serving many purposes, not the least of which was a "butler" of sorts that she used at breakfast and dinner to put her plate of food on to roll back to the table at the vast River Valley Retirement Village where she and Chris had lived for the past five years since leaving Florida.

A long and successful career in real estate since he retired from the Air Force, Chris had done his due diligence in selecting a place to live. They chose River Valley from a short list of other facilities and had settled in nicely on the fourth floor with new friends from all walks of life.

Another clap of thunder startled Jane a bit and she pushed herself off the bed, not wanting to make any noise. Grabbing a small glass of water from the kitchen she made her way into the living room, through the dark to the chair that was near the large glass patio doors and sat in silence watching the show nature was presenting. Now and then a flash of light from the sky would illuminate the small framed picture next to the patio doors. It was an image of the ocean taken in Florida before she and Chris closed that chapter of their lives. She had loved the smell of the salt air living near the beach; the weather at times was an aid to her aching legs.

Sipping her water, she noticed a small shoe box on the tray next to her chair that she had put there just a couple days before. The box contained so much of her past. It was a bittersweet experience each and every time she removed the lid. It was her sole portal to yesterday, filled with pictures of family and friends, many now long departed from her life, alive now only in memory and thought.

Mama and Papa were in that box, along with her brothers Karl and Nocki. Her precious young friend Avi was in the box as well along with her first husband Max and countless relatives. Black and white images from another time, other places and lives that Jane had lived.

Carefully she pulled open the box, knowing full well the flood of memories that would come forth. A flash of light streaked across the sky highlighting for a moment the first picture of Jane at age six and a half, with a broad smile, short hair, and her hands on the wooden handle of a scooter in front of the stone apartment building they called home.

Turning on a small reading light next to her chair Jane flipped over the picture. Her eyes adjusted to the small lamp light, and she read the words she had written on the back of the picture…

"Me...Munich 1934."

Jane gazed at the image of herself from more than eighty-three years ago and quietly muttered under her breath, *"Oh, mein Gott, so sehr vor langer Zeit."* (Oh, my God, so very long ago.)

Holding the picture, she sat very still and listened to the steady rain pelting the window of their condo. As the ebb and flow of the thunder and lightning filled the living room she began to think about how many storms she had endured in her eighty-nine years on the planet.

Jane slowly ran her fingers over the edges of the pictures in the box. Each one a messenger from another time, each and every one a snapshot of her past. She thought about the blessings that came from her family and faith. How she learned from a very young age that obstacles were meant to be overcome.

Jane went deep within herself and remembered a time when the world was a far different place and yet, as the years had taught her, still the same in so very many ways. Looking back at the photograph of herself a single tear escaped and ran down her cheek.

Then Jane smiled and began to recall her journey, as a little girl in worn torn Munich, Germany under Hitler, making her way to America, her long battle with MS and, most importantly, how her faith in God had become the rudder that steered her through all of it.

As the rain came down at a steady pace, the heavy drops created a lullaby of sorts by pounding down on the padded deck chair on the porch and bringing about a sense of peace to Jane.

"I've always loved thunderstorms," she whispered to herself in the dark. As she promptly nodded off to sleep in the big chair her subconscious mind began to peel back the layers of her life.

16

CHAPTER ONE

"Bing...Bing...Bing"

In a daze Jane quickly closed the door to the doctor's office behind her and made her way through a maze of medical offices to the lobby. Pushing through the revolving door, she found herself standing on the sidewalk, her mind reeling from the words delivered to her just moments ago by Dr. Musser.

"You have multiple sclerosis."

This early spring morning in 1967 had begun without any hint of the impeding diagnosis that would change her life. She stood there in the March sunshine recalling what just transpired a few moments ago.

Jane had been admitted to the hospital recently for "vestibular neuritis" which is an abnormality of the inner ear, but the doctor now boldly pronounced it was multiple sclerosis. As his words hung in the air between them, she instantly pushed back, every fiber of her being crying out, "NO! This is a mistake! A missed test or something! Anything but this!"

Her mind whirled as she recalled the conversation moments before. "Are you absolutely sure, Doctor?" Jane pleaded. "It must be something else, it can't be that," she insisted. "It just can't be that," she mumbled as her voice trailed off.

Sitting behind his desk Dr. Musser surveyed her response to his diagnosis with kind, but steadfast eyes.

After a few moments of silence, Jane lifted her head and with a voice full of resignation, she asked, "What is the prognosis for me? What will happen to me?"

Dr. Musser leaned back in his chair and said, "I can't give you a prognosis, Jane. This disease has no set course of symptoms and it affects every patient differently. It could go *Bing, Bing, Bing,*" he said, snapping his fingers as he spoke those three short words, "and you could be in a wheelchair."

He continued to explain more about MS but Jane could no longer hear him. As he spoke, Dr. Musser seemed to suddenly start shrinking behind his formidable desk and moving away from her into the far corner of his office as if she was looking at him through the wrong end of a telescope.

He was still talking when Jane stood straight up and simply started walking out the door in stunned silence.

She felt like a death sentence had just been handed her. Jane kept on walking, staring into nothingness until she found herself on the sidewalk.

A passing stranger snapped her back into reality.

"Are you alright, Miss?"

Jane silently nodded to him, quietly walked to her car in the parking lot and with a mighty force slammed the car door, wishing she could shut out the last few moments of her life from her mind.

The short drive back to the Blue Cross Blue Shield office where she worked was a blur, and Jane was thankful for an open parking spot in front of the office on Fourteenth Street. She sat for a moment in the car and checked her watch which showed one o'clock indicating that her lunch hour was over.

"Worst lunch I've ever had," she thought to herself.

She made her way to the little glassed-in cubby hole office in the subscriber service section where she worked and noticed the subscribers seated, waiting to see the next available agent.

Jane was barely settled back in her cubicle when the desk telephone rang. Taking a deep breath and with as much poise as she could muster, Jane answered, "Yes, Marie?"

"Mr. Sylvester here to see you, Mrs. Horten," Marie the receptionist replied.

Jane forced a smile and said, "Send him right in."

Oh no, she thought. Not today, he is so long-winded and always so sad. Her already clouded mind had no room for Carlos Sylvester and his problems. She quickly pushed her misgivings aside and greeted him with a smile.

"Well hello, Mr. Sylvester, come right in and have a seat," Jane offered. "What can I do for you today?"

Carlos looked down at his hands folded neatly in his lap and said, "It's my wife. She's not getting any better. She can't even feed herself anymore. Sometimes I just wish she would die." Realizing his last words, he suddenly looked up at Jane, but quickly remembering his place he continued, "She is slowly running out of nursing home days, too. Maybe you could tell me how many days she has left?" Carlos asked hopefully.

"Yes, yes of course I'll check for you, Mr. Sylvester." Jane picked up the phone and requested the records. When the clerk handed her a thick file Jane looked through the paperwork of Hilda Sylvester. She was stunned when she saw the diagnosis… *Multiple Sclerosis*.

Jane dug her fingernails deep into the flesh of her tightly clenched fists. Her first thought was about how long Mrs. Sylvester had the disease. She scanned over the pages while Carlos sat quietly just a few feet away.

There it was. The date of onset was 1964, just three years earlier. In that moment, Dr. Musser's words flashed through her mind. "No set course, *Bing, Bing, Bing*, wheelchair, nursing home."

The case of Hilda Sylvester was confirming his pronouncement less than an hour before. Up until that point Jane was unaware of Hilda's diagnosis. Previous visits from Mr. Sylvester were mostly about himself and how he suffered having to take care of his beloved, but there was never any mention by him of what the disease was and no cause to open the files until today when he inquired about nursing home coverage.

Jane felt a sudden surge of empathy for Carlos and Hilda, no longer just names on a file, no longer just a man who talked too much and carried around such deep sadness on his back like a ton of bricks.

Jane couldn't wait to bring the interview to a close. She regained her senses, answered all of Mr. Sylvester's questions as quickly as possible, and with great compassion bid him a pleasant afternoon.

Once he left her cubicle Jane simply sat in silence. The events of the day settling in on her like a wet overcoat and there was a weight on her shoulders and ache in her heart that had not been there for a very long time.

CHAPTER TWO

The Search

The weekend traffic in Wilmington, Delaware is notoriously hectic, and this Friday afternoon was no exception. Traffic was bumper to bumper giving Jane time to think about the events of the day.

As she slowly inched forward in the line of cars around Augustine Cut Off, Jane said quietly to herself, "What are the odds that Carlos Sylvester's wife has the same disease that I've been diagnosed with just hours ago?"

Suddenly she remembered that a small neighborhood library was located in the area. "Maybe I can find some answers there," she announced in a much stronger voice. Through the open car window, she spied a sign with an arrow on it and large, age-faded letters that spelled out "Library."

Jane made her move, pulled off the main throughway to a little traveled side street where the small but well stocked library that she had visited a time or two was located. There could be something, maybe books, or articles, or research papers, anything at all that might shed some light on the mysterious disease called multiple sclerosis.

Although she was very tired and her body was screaming for her to hurry home, lie down, and get some rest, the need to find out whatever she could about MS was greater than her exhaustion. The reality of MS had been suddenly forced upon her in one unforgettable instant and even though it was now part of her being, she was not ready to accept it.

The tension welled up inside her.

"I'm only 38 years old! I am too young to just lie down and give up without a fight!" she shouted in despair. Her words hung in the air as both a warning and a declaration, but Jane was the only one who could hear them.

She pulled up in front of the North Wilmington Library just as it was about to close. She got in with just minutes to spare and was greeted by a kindly old man with gray hair and a permanently lopsided smile.

"I know you are about to close, but I need something, anything at all that is published on multiple sclerosis." Jane said. Her words sounded hurried and desperate.

With one hand, the old man behind the counter rubbed his gray-bristled chin and shaking his head conveyed his answer, almost before Jane finished her question.

"I am so sorry. We have nothing in print on MS," He said. *"But"* he quickly added with a distinct note of empathy in his voice as if trying to console her in some way. "There is much research going on you know." He then took a deep breath and continued speaking, "The National MS Society says that the interrupted letters of the MS logo will one day, and hopefully very soon, be totally closed up and show the logo in bold, uninterrupted letters."

"When that day comes, it will signify that the puzzle of MS has been solved and a cure is on the way," he insisted, showing his crooked, but friendly smile.

Jane shook her head as if to try and understand his words, but they seemed hollow and far away. How was it possible that this man knew so much about MS? Did he have personal knowledge of the disease? Was someone close to him stricken...perhaps even himself? Jane decided to browse through the shelves for a few minutes. Her fingers found a copy of *Psycho-Cybernetics* by Maxwell Maltz, a surgeon who had created a system of ideas that he claimed could improve one's image and in turn that person could lead a more successful and fulfilling life.

"Hmm," said the old man at the checkout counter. "Good book, but not on MS. Best of luck to you, Miss," he called out to Jane as she hurriedly left the small library. While the library was devoid of information she was seeking, this man was a messenger of sorts, saying what she needed to hear, at just the right moment.

Making her way home, Jane pulled her faded blue 1952 Studebaker onto Mayflower Drive and dragged her exhausted body up a couple of flights of stairs on legs that felt like two buckets of cement. Ignoring the numbness and prickly sensations in her lower torso, she unlocked the front door with a deep sigh of relief and said out loud, "It's good to be home."

After sitting for a few minutes to regain a measure of strength, Jane picked through her meager supply of victuals in the refrigerator, opting for some cheese and crackers, a large glass of milk, and small glass of wine from a remnant bottle of Dubonnet. Without enough energy to even turn on the television, Jane let out an exaggerated sigh and let herself fall into her favorite easy chair by the window.

Within moments a flurry of thoughts started whirring through her mind like a raging storm. Waves of despair crashed over and over again drenching Jane with an overwhelming sense of dread that eventually subsided, leaving behind one question that kept repeating itself and stood out among so many others. "What will become of me?" Jane cried out from her chair. "What about my future" she said out loud, more of a statement than a question.

But soon many questions came forth. What would her life be like as the wife of U.S. Air Force Major Chris Johnson, whom she hoped to marry when his tour in Vietnam ended in a year? What will happen when Chris finds out I have MS? Will all my hopes and dreams come to an end?

The storm in her mind began to swirl again, so many more unanswered questions began to surface from a place of fear inside her. The questions were too deep and far too terrifying to even try and deal with now.

Jane sat back in the chair, closed her eyes and wondered…where and when did this all start? She began to dig into the deep recesses of her mind for something, anything at all that would give some clues as to how all of this happened.

Did the MS start when she was a child? Was she born with it? Did it start when she was a young girl?

"How can I find out?" She wondered out loud.

Jane was determined to dig as deep as needed to make sense of this senseless illness that was taking her hostage from within. She began to pull on the deep roots of her very existence, going back to the beginning, looking and searching for answers.

CHAPTER THREE

Angel of Peace

Jane Raber announced her cry of arrival into the world on December 3, 1928. She was only two 1/2 pounds and was born with a ruptured hernia. Hans and Karola Raber were overjoyed to have a girl join their family after having two sons, but there were some serious concerns about her health because lifesaving incubators had not yet been invented. Baby Jane would endure four grueling Alpine winters before doctors pronounced her strong enough to undergo an operation that would close her ruptured hernia.

On many occasions in the ensuing years Mama would often smile at her daughter in absolute wonderment and pronounce, "Jane, mein Liebchen, (my darling,) you are one of God's walking miracles!" "I know Mama," Jane would always answer, with a very big smile on her face. "You said it's because God loves me."

"Yes, he does Janchen and look at you now, already eight years old and growing like a weed!"

It was 1936 and Adolf Hitler had been sworn in as chancellor just three years prior and in 36 months Germany would be set on a collision course with the rest of the world.[1]

But for now, Jane's world was about the simple wonders of life.

"Mama, after we finish our homework, can Nocki, Karl, and I go to the English Garden? We would like to go see the Monopteros, you know, the Greek ruins?"

Mama thought for a moment and said, "Yes children, you may go, but be home by six o'clock for dinner."

It was a fine spring day and the trees were in full bloom and everything seemed new and exciting. It was a short five-minute walk to the English Garden and as they got closer to Prinzregenten Street and the start of the vast garden Karl cried out, "Oh look! Circus Krone is advertising a new show!"

Jane chimed in, "Look! Up the street a man on stilts carrying a big sign!" "And, he is at least ten meters tall!" Nocki shouted with a greatly exaggerated exuberance.

---

[1] A steady Nazi program of socialism was designed to bring back a forgotten pride to the 127 million ethnic Germans after the crushing defeat of World War I and the subsequent Treaty of Versailles. Just two months after Hitler took power, Dachau, the first Nazi concentration camp was opened on March 22, 1933 just outside of Munich where the Raber family lived.

"THE FLYING WALLENDAS," The sign loudly proclaimed.

Unable to hold back their excitement at the spectacle unfolding before them the children broke out into a fast run as they spied a bicycle driving across a rope tied between two trees.

When they looked up at the trees they saw a handsome man, who they later learned was the great Karl Wallenda, performing a mini high-wire act. Two of his sons were hanging outstretched on either side of a pole draped across Wallenda's broad shoulders. Moving in slow motion they changed into different ballet positions as their father peddled across the wire.

"Oh, look, there is Sepp," said Karl as he sprinted over to stand next to his friend.

"Hi Karl," said Sepp. "Say have you ever had a Coca-Cola?"

"Why, no I haven't," said Karl as his brother and sister crowded around him.

"Well, you better go buy one at the kiosk over there, just near the end of the Wallenda's high-wire rope" urged

Sepp. "They're only five pfennigs."

Karl looked around at his siblings for support but Jane and Nocki just shrugged their shoulders, indicating they had no money either.

"Oh, what the heck," chirped Sepp, "have a sip of mine, but only a small sip, Karl."

Karl pushed the glass bottle to his lips and tilted his head slightly. He barely tasted the cold soda before Sepp grabbed the bottle.

"THATS ENOUGH," he barked.

Sepp handed the brown glass bottle to both Jane and Nocki, who also took the smallest of sips.

"WELL?" demanded Sepp in high expectation, "What do you think? Did you like it?"

"Ja, it was okay," said Karl.

"How about you, Jane?" asked Sepp. "Did you like the Coca-Cola?"

Jane crinkled up her nose as she answered, "I didn't like it. It tickled my nose!" Nocki had no opinion other than "Ah…it's okay I guess."

Sepp spoke up again and said, "My uncle who has been to America not once but twice said that Coca-Cola tastes so much better in a glass with lots of ice in it."

Jane was becoming bored with the Coca-Cola conversation when she saw "Black Mari." She was a tall, beautiful Gypsy girl with flowing coal black hair, dark eyes, and wore earrings that hung down to her shoulders on golden chains dangling two beaded red raspberries.

Jane had always wanted to reach out and touch those beautiful earrings that Mari always wore...*just once*. Instead she greeted her friend with a hearty, "Hi Mari!"

"Hello Jane," came Mari's quiet response.

"Did you see the Flying Wallendas? They are going to be at the Circus Krone," Jane gushed.

"I know," said Mari, glancing around nervously with a faraway look in her eyes. "I need to hurry on," she said, her graphite eyes fearfully darting in all directions.

"We mustn't be seen talking together. It's dangerous for you and dangerous for me," Mari warned.

With that Mari spun around and rushed as fast as her spiked heels would carry her west up Prinzregenten Street in the direction of the Angel of Peace, a most audacious, gilded monument perched atop a very tall, round column resting on a large, four-sided tapered pedestal.

Jane stood in place stunned at the words Mari spoke. A feeling of deep regret covered her like a blanket because she longed to know Mari better, to understand her customs and culture, and it appeared that was all but lost. A sense of helplessness crept in as she didn't understand what Mari meant by "dangerous," but decided that perhaps because she really didn't know her, she might have been snooty and perhaps quite strange.

Jane turned her eyes to the Angel of Peace. She always loved looking at the glorious, golden angel with a long, wind-blown billowing skirt who looked down across the River Isar from her lofty perch. She represented the 25 peaceful years after the Franco-German war of 1870-71 and since 1896 her arms were outstretched to all of Munich, holding an ornate, gilded olive branch in one hand and a statue of the Greek goddess of wisdom, handicraft, and war, Pallas Athene in the other.

"*Dangerous?*" she thought to herself, still not quite sure what to think or feel about her conversation with Mari.

Then a voice called out to her, interrupting her thought process. "JANE!"

"Oh. Hi, Hedwig." Jane said with a hint of a smile.

"Jane! Jane! I SAW HIM! MY BOYFRIEND!" Hedwig giggled. Hedwig's exuberance was completely opposite Mari's fearfulness and was refreshingly light.

"And, where did you see him?" Jane quipped.

"I saw him at Café Luitpold. I saw him right through the big windows, there where all the guests were having coffee and cake. He was singing with a megaphone you know. We can go there now and I will show you," Hedwig proudly proclaimed.

At that very moment, the bells of St. Anne's Catholic Church chimed six times, the sound ringing off the stone walls, echoing across Munich as the daylight started to dwindle.

"Oh, no I can't," cried Jane. "It's six o'clock and we have to go home!"

"Karl! Nocki!" Jane called out, looking for her brothers. "We have to go now, we cannot be late for supper."

The three Raber children broke out into a run, each determined to be the first in the door, but Jane turned back to her friend shouting, "You better go home as well Hedwig. It's supper time!"

Jane took one more backward glance at the Angel of Peace before joining her brothers in their race back home. Something deep inside her insisted she remember this moment because while she didn't know it then, Jane would need her angels in the days and months to come.

CHAPTER FOUR

The Radio

The seasons came and went, Frühling (Spring), Sommer (Summer), Herbst (Autumn), und Winter in the Bavarian capitol of Munich and the excited shouts of *"Frohe Weihnachten und ein glückliches Neues Jahr!"* (Merry Christmas and a Happy New Year!) rang out as the bells of St. Anne's Church pealed in the holiday season and snow blanketed the streets and rooftops.

Life for most Germans went on as usual, as they began to enjoy a resurgence of their heritage, but for the Jews it was another story.

There was a palpable fear in Munich as the Nazi party began to expand and recruit. Jews who lived there had begun to see a systematic "erasing" of their lives beginning in 1935 with the enactment of The Nuremberg Laws that stripped Jews of their citizenship, excluded them from many jobs and government positions. They were not allowed to ride on street cars or sit on park benches reserved for "Aryans." Jewish and German children were being kept apart by their parents and the fascist rhetoric that spewed from Adolf Hitler on the radio fanned the flames of hate.

It was now 1938 and two years had passed since The Flying Wallendas had performed at the Circus Krone, and since Jane had seen Mari's dangling earrings.

"Mama, look the sleeves on my coat are getting too short," lamented Jane. "Yes, I know," Mama answered. "The sleeves are the same length but your arms are growing." Mama laughed, "I will have to make the necessary alterations on your coat and also the boys' pants." she sighed. "They will have to do for another year."

Hans Raber turned the key in the lock of his front door and the aroma of his favorite dinner permeated his nostrils. On the other side of the kitchen door Mama was busy preparing a dinner of sauerkraut, knockwurst, and *stadtbrot*, one of Munich's most popular breads and an absolute staple for many Bavarian households.

Jane and her brothers were occupied in the far corner of the large kitchen by the balcony window. They were having a fun time manipulating their favorite wooden puppet heads that Papa had carved for them, along with a folding "window theater" mimicking their own version of a "Punch and Judy" puppet show.

"Come now, Children, put your toys away and wash up for dinner. Papa is home, you must have heard him putting his bicycle away in the hall."

"*Grüess Gott*, Papa!" (God's Greetings!) Jane chirped as she sprinted toward her father while blurting out, "Do you know who I saw today, Papa?"

"*Grüess Gott*, Jane," replied Papa as he patted her head. "No, I do not know. Whom did you see today?"

"I saw Dr. Weiser today" she proclaimed. "I had a check-up and no cavities! See my teeth are cleaned! See how they sparkle, Papa!" Jane proudly tilted up her chin to show off her teeth in a broad smile. "You made a violin for Dr. Weiser, Papa, he said he needs you now to come and fix it for him."

"What? Again?" chuckled Papa. "I was just there last week, I think he probably just needs another violin lesson, but I will go and see him tomorrow."

Hans was a violin maker, like his father before him who was highly respected for his skills in making stringed instruments and as a purveyor to the court of King Ludwig

II.

King Ludwig was only eighteen when his father died after a three-day illness, and he ascended the Bavarian throne. Though Bavaria retained a degree of autonomy on some matters within the new German Reich, Ludwig increasingly withdrew from day-to-day affairs of state in favor of extravagant artistic and architectural projects. He was a devoted patron of the composer Richard Wagner. The two often rode in the gondola on the small lake within the castle, not only for their own muse, but also for "dreaming up" *Der Ring des Nibelungen* (*The Ring of the Nibelungen, a series of five operas by Wagner*).

Hans Raber Sr. had made a name for himself while working for the King and he passed along his legacy, skills, and craft to his son which in turn gave him a position of great respect. It was that respect that allowed Papa and Mama to secure the apartment in a five-story building that was owned by and housed Jews. The landlady admitted the non-Jewish Raber family to her building; honored to have Hans Raber as a tenant.

"Pass me the loaf of bread, Karl," requested Papa. "I

want to carve up some slices to go with this fine meal your Mama has prepared for us." The usual dinner conversation began.

"How was school today?" Papa asked.

Nocki was most anxious to be the first to report to his father.

"Herr Goetz held up my colored paper composition before the whole class today and then he tacked it up on the cork tablet on the wall for everyone to see!" blurted Nocki, now in the sixth grade. "It will be there tomorrow, too" he said showing off a toothy but very proud smile.

"That is very commendable, Nocki" his father lauded. "Keep up the good work."

"Papa, Karl, and I ran into Hedwig today, you remember she is the neighborhood *"blödl"* (nitwit)", added Jane.

"Hoppla!" (Hold it!) Papa cut in with a stern warning. "There will be no name calling. Hedwig is a very sweet person and good soul. She is a very likeable young lady despite her mental handicap."

"Yes Papa," Jane said quickly and contritely and then continued, "She had a whole pfennig in her pocket and gave it to Karl to keep but we went to Frau Steinberger's candy shop and she gave us a whole, long piece of licorice, must have been a meter long!" Jane said. "I broke it into three pieces, one for me, one for Karl, and one for Hedwig."

Papa began to eat his dinner when Jane spoke again, "Papa?"

"Yes, Jane?"

"Why can't we have money and buy candy every day too?" she asked while biting into her bread, her brothers with their mouths full, nodding in enthusiastic agreement.

"Well," answered their father thoughtfully, "This question will have to be taken up with your mother, she manages the hausfrau purse. Plus, if you ate candy every day next time you see Dr. Weiser your check-up might not be so good."

"Eat your dinner children before it gets cold," Mama admonished, instantly delaying any further money discussions for the moment. But it would become a subject Papa and Mama would soon have to deal with.

While Mama and the children cleared away the dishes, Papa turned the radio on for the local news, but instead the voice of Germany's "Führer" filled the air. Adolf Hitler was shouting in his usual bellicose manner, about the "rabble in our midst" having to be exterminated. The propaganda message Hitler was delivering had undoubtedly been created by Joseph Goebbels, Germany's "Minister of Enlightenment and Propaganda", a position he relished.

Radio had become the primary delivery system for messages of socialism, patriotism and Aryan pride throughout Germany.[2] Mama hurriedly opened the balcony door and shouted back, "Hurry Hans! Turn the volume all the way up so that our Jewish friends and neighbors can listen in! You know they have no radios since they were confiscated a few days ago when the Gestapo came through all the apartments and took them.

The balconies slowly began to fill up with people. Next door lived the Gottschalks, their balcony so close it was within arm's reach. On their balcony Jane and her brothers

---

[2] All homes that had a radio had to pay two marks a month to pay for the cost of the broadcasts. To ensure that all German households had a radio, Goebbels arranged for production of two cheap types of radios, priced at 35 and 72 marks and they were known as "The People's Receivers."

often positioned one of their puppet heads for fun on the iron spikes normally used for holding ropes for drying the laundry. Herr and Frau Walhaus lived on the third floor. One floor below lived Herr and Frau Hirsch and the Rotter sisters who were always dressed in black. "They are Rabbis," explained Mama when the children asked about how they dressed. Mama was helpful to their neighbors because every Friday, their Jewish Sabbath, she would light fires for heat in all the Jewish orthodox households upstairs.

Mama called them her *"Sabbat Aufgaben"* (Sabbath Duties) as she took her work very seriously and counted it as a privilege to serve all the Jewish families in the building, whenever she was needed.

As night began to close in on Munich Hitler's voice barking from the radio made the impending darkness seem even more foreboding.

"Alles ist in Ordnung! Deutschland ist unbesiegbar, es ist eine Weltmacht!" (Everything is in order now! Germany is invincible, it is a world power!) *"Diejenigen unter uns die sich unwürdig dieses grosssen Landes fühlen müssen beseitigt werden!"* (Those among us who are undeserving of

this great land must be eliminated!) *"Allem was die Menschen nachstreben als ein höheres Ziel, sei es Religion, Sozialismus, Demokratie, es ist für den Juden nur Mittel zum Zweck, die Art und Weise, seine Gier nach Gold und Herrschaft zu befriedigen!"* (Everything men strive after as a higher goal, be it religion, socialism, democracy, is to the Jew only a means to an end, the way to satisfy his lust for gold and domination.)

Hitler pounded the desk where he stood and screamed into the microphone, *"In seinen Auswirkungen und Konsequenzen der Juden ist er wie eine rassische Tuberkulose der Nationen!!"* (In his effects and consequences, The Jew is like a racial tuberculosis of the nations!!)

The Führer paused for effect and then yelled in his high-pitched voice, *"Das letztendliche Ziel muss jedoch der unwiderrufliche Ausbau der Juden sein!"* (The ultimate objective must, however, be the irrevocable removal of the Jews!)

Papa and Mama pulled the children close and stood in silence as Hitler's words bounced off the concrete walls and watched as their friends and neighbors went back into their homes and quietly closed the balcony doors behind them.

Not long after that broadcast, Karl thought he would scare the Gottschalks and put out a devil head puppet on a spike. When Jane glanced out of the window to see if Frau Gottschalk hung out a towel with a happy face painted on it in response to the puppet as she usually did, she called her family to the balcony. This night the Gottschalks window was totally covered by a black cloth.

"All of Germany hears the Führer with the People's Receiver."

CHAPTER FIVE

Max and Moritz

Life in Munich for Jane was exciting as it could be for a young girl, even as the darkening clouds of the Nazi Party began to cast long shadows across Germany.

Jane had a wonderful little friend named Avi. Both girls were nine years old and enjoyed each other's company a great deal. They had always played together on the sidewalk in front of their apartment, but now they were no longer allowed to be seen in public together as Avi was Jewish and Jane of the Christian faith. While neither girl understood why that should matter, their playground was now confined to a fair sized, stone tile court yard located just below the five-story apartment building where they lived. They couldn't even go to the movies, even though the movie theater was just next door, for fear that someone might see them and alert the Gestapo. There was always the *"Gauleiter"* (a political official governing a district under Nazi rule) around whom the children dubbed the neighborhood *"spitzel"* or "snitch."

His job was to report any anti-Nazi activity to the Gestapo.

It was a tenuous time as neighbors betrayed each other to gain favor, schoolchildren reported on classmates, managers spied on employees, and there was no safe place as any bit of information, real or imagined could be incriminating and lead to dire consequences.

The big stone walls which separated each courtyard from the other neighbors was very high, which not only afforded some privacy, but also protection from prying eyes. Avi and Jane decided to make the stone tiled courtyard their playground.

The girls shared their favorite toys. For Jane, it was her treasured boy doll named Gottlieb, dressed in a true Bavarian lederhosen outfit, and for Avi it was the two little frogs that her mother had given her on her ninth birthday she named Max and Mortiz.

The girls would giggle in delight watching Max hop around the stone tiles with Moritz not far behind, their big eyes and shiny skin making them look cartoon-like.

But today something seemed different, puzzling, and ominous when Avi said, "Soon my family and I will be going away."

Jane stopped watching the little amphibians darting back and forth on the white tile and asked, "But Avi where are you going and when will you come back?"

Avi hung her head, pushed back her hair from her eyes, looked at Jane and said, "Not for a long time."

With that Avi solemnly scooped up Max while Jane scrambled to grab Mortiz who was hopping towards the far corner of the courtyard. Finally, Jane caught the frog and the girls returned them both to their terrarium.

The girls stopped, looked at each other for a moment and then Avi simply left. Jane watched her friend walking away carrying her two little green pets and felt an indescribable sadness in her young heart.

Jane did not understand.

Later that evening, the Raber family was unusually quiet around the dinner table. The banter and conversation had grown less and less as the Nazi activity in Germany became more frequent.

Around six o'clock there was a soft knock at the front door. Mama approached the door quietly and peered out the peephole.

"Oh, its Frau Hirsch and Avi," cried Mama and flung the door open wide for them to enter. "Hurry come in, Frau Hirsch, before somebody sees us."

Frau Hirsch smiled and replied timidly, "No, better not Frau Raber, Avi just wanted to give Jane a present." And with that Avi held out her most treasured possession, the little terrarium, to Jane.

Jane said in a hushed voice, "Oh my, it's Max and Moritz!"

The two girls hugged each other for what seemed like a long time, neither wanting to let go of the other. Suddenly Jane broke away and returned with Gottlieb and held out the doll to Avi, who hugged it tight.

There were no tears when Jane announced, "I will take good care of Max and Mortiz until you get back, Avi. And Gottlieb will take care of you."

Frau Hirsch, sensing that the moment needed to end, looked around with great apprehension and without a word seized Avi's hand and together they scurried back to their upstairs apartment.

As the door closed behind them, Jane put the terrarium in a safe place in her bedroom. Little did she know that just 48 hours later one of the most horrible events in the history of the German Jews would send shock waves around the world nor did she have a thought that she would never see her beloved Avi again.

CHAPTER SIX

The Market

As was long the custom, women in German households went shopping every morning for items needed for the day's meals and so it was in Jane's neighborhood of Lehel, which was regarded as "the oldest suburb of Munich," located near the center of the city. As soon as the shops opened at 8 a.m. the streets would fill with the *Hausfrauen* (housewives) who could be seen making their appointed rounds to the butcher, baker, dairy shop, and vegetable market. It was during these daily excursions that the Hausfrauen would take time out on their shopping trips to connect with friends on the street and catch up on local gossip. Now talk was more plentiful than food, as the times were getting very sparse economically.

They would also talk politics and voice complaints, but even those conversations had become sparse as few dared to speak out loud as to the rising tensions in Germany for fear of repercussions.

"It's eight o'clock, Jane! Get up!" Mama commanded from the kitchen. "It's time to get going. It's Saturday you know." She added impatiently, "The shops will fill up fast and you know how I hate to wait in long lines."

Jane rubbed the sleep from her eyes and glanced at Max and Mortiz who were watching her with unblinking frog eyes from inside their little glass box. "Yes, Mama, I am coming," she answered. She bolted along the semi-dark corridor past the bedrooms until something hit her hard in the face!

"OUCH!" Jane cried out in pain. "Those boys! They are always so careless and leave the exercise rings hanging instead of replacing them on the wall hooks! I could have broken my nose, teeth, or worse," she blurted out in a voice full of accusation.

Mama rushed out of the kitchen, down the hall, around the corner, and turned on the hall light to see Jane standing there with her white gloved hands covering her face.

After a quick inspection Mama determined that her daughter was not badly hurt and only would have a small bruise on her forehead as a reminder.

"One day your father will have to take these rings down," Mama said taking Jane's side for just a moment as she looked up at the high ceiling where they were attached. Smoothing back a lock of dark hair from her face, she continued, "Don't be so hard on your brothers, Jane. The last time the tables were turned and you left the rings hanging...remember?"

She smiled at the thought and as her mother adjusted her white gloves, Jane did the same and off they went to the market. It was less than ten minutes before they crossed paths with Frau Gersten.

"Oh my," Mama said, under her breath. "Here comes the chatterbox. She is a bit of a silly goose, but we'll just try and ignore her Jane," as she tugged at her daughter's hand and chuckled as they pressed on.

"*Guten Morgen* Frau Raber," barked the woman.

"Good Morning, Frau Gersten," answered Mama. "*Schöner Tag, heute, nicht wahr?*" (Beautiful day, isn't it?)

Frau Gersten placed her hands on her hips and loudly announced, "Well not such a beautiful day for me." "Herr Nagelschmitt at the coal distributing house just informed me that I can no longer have my usual supply of two thousand pounds of coal for the winter and that I can only buy half this year!"

"Yes, yes, I know," Mama agreed. "It is terrible, and I hear we will be rationed shoes and gasoline as well."

"*I don't need gasoline!*" snapped Frau Gersten. "We don't have a Volkswagen, only the very rich can afford them anyway." Ignoring Mama's attempt to move away, she added. "I do hear that it's getting easier to afford one," she said in hopes of continuing the conversation.

"Yes," said Mama, half turning back to the woman. "Our neighbors, the Gottschalks just bought a Volkswagen and…"

"ACH!" spat Frau Gersten, interrupting Mama in mid-sentence. "They are Jewish! They have all the money and they can afford it!" She continued on, "I don't know what is going to happen to the Jews anyway and somehow I am a bit terrified of that. My husband said the Führer will send them all to back to Palestina." "Besides," she prattled on, "It is pretty good what our Führer is doing!" She then pounded her prominent big bosomed chest and declared, "Just look! I

58

received my *Ehrenkreuz der Deutschen Mutter* (German Mother's Cross[3]) for having ten children and I also get all the milk I need for free. I can use that alright," she snickered.

Frau Gersten proudly wore the cross as if she was a personal friend of Adolf Hitler.

"Besides my girls all got new BDM uniforms" (Hitler Youth Movement for girls) she clucked. "Oh yes, make no mistake about it, Hitler is good for Germany," she postured, shaking a thick finger in Mama's face, her voice raising up and drawing attention from others in the market place.

"I will have no one say anything contrary to that," she bellowed.

Jane stood there waiting for her mother to respond, after what seemed an eternity Mama, somewhat shaken yet managing to smile said, "Oh no, no, no. I think you should get everything coming to you, Frau Gersten."

---

[3] The crosses were a decoration instituted by the Führer in December, 1938 and given out on both Mother's Day and August 4th, which was the birthday of Hitler's mother as an incentive to encourage the growth of an Aryan nation. In the period before World War II more than 3 million crosses were handed out and seldom were they refused. In Nazi Germany the women who wore the crosses had to prove they were of a pure Aryan background and that brought with it respect from the civil service and they were also granted seats on public transportation.

With that, Mama spun on her heels, turned to face her daughter and with a wink said, "Come Jane, we must continue on with our shopping." As they carted off down the street, Frau Gersten had already moved in on another Hausfrau and was exhorting the power and glory of the Third Reich and how Hitler was going to change the world for the better.

CHAPTER SEVEN

Kristallnacht

It was just about eight o'clock in the evening on the ninth of November 1938. The family was settled in for the night when suddenly Papa and Mama and the children heard what seemed to be a loud commotion coming from the hallway and, as if in one choregraphed movement, they all crowded together to peer out a small slit opening at the door. They could see men in Nazi uniforms with their shiny black boots tramping up the stairs creating a haunting echo.

"Get away from the door," cried Papa, in a loud yet muffled tone. "It's the Gestapo!"

Mama ushered the family into the living room and ordered them not to say a word about what was happening. Mama left the children and went back for another look through the peephole in the door just in time to see the Hirsch's and many other neighbors herded into a large vehicle that was waiting on the street.

What Mama saw next froze her heart.

Through the open door at the Gottschalks apartment across the hall she saw what seemed to be two silver colored elongated metal containers that were used to transport dead bodies.

In shock, Mama chocked back her tears and slowly turned away from the door, her face a mirror of fear. She tightly clasped her hands together and with her eyes closed she uttered to herself, *"Sie töteten sich"* (They killed themselves.)

Black booted men one on each end of the boxes carried the Gottschalks away, as they would a container of trash. Papa and Mama looked at their frightened family huddled together before them.

"Never talk to anyone about what took place tonight," Mama warned. Seeing Nocki's tear stained face, she put her arms around him and with a mixture of stern gentleness said, *"Keine Tränen, mein Sohn, keine Diskussionen, auch nicht unter Familie."* (No tears my son, no discussions, not even among the family.)

"Ja, Kinder, leider ist das heute so, man muss aufpassen was man sagt, denn Wände haben Ohren," (Yes, Children, regretfully it is so today, one must use extreme caution about what one says, even walls have ears,) murmured

Hans.

There was not much sleep to be had the rest of the night.

It would become known as *"Kristallnacht"* (Night of Broken Glass[4]) and by the next morning the news was spreading fast that all the Jewish businesses, synagogues, and schools had been destroyed.

The rampage was a complete and horrendous destruction of people's lives and properties. The streets looked empty, almost ghostly, except for the looters who came with large baskets to fill with stolen goods, picked clean from those who once were neighbors but now were nothing more than a memory. For Jane it would also mark the beginning of many years of recurring nightmares that always started with those same, horrible eyes appearing in the distance. They began just as dots, growing larger and larger as they approached

---

[4] Early reports put the number of dead at the hands of the Nazi's at ninety-one, but when deaths from post-arrest mistreatment and suicides were added in the number climbed into the hundreds. Over 1,000 synagogues were burned to the ground and over 7,000 Jewish businesses were either totally destroyed or damaged throughout Germany.

her until they became huge, and those eyes would be staring at her.

In her sleep she lay rigid, frozen in place. and whispered to herself, *"Nichts sagen, nichts denken, nicht rühren bis die Augen vorbei gegangen sind, dass sie dir nichts antun koennen."* (Say nothing, think nothing, don't even move until the eyes have gone past so they will not harm you.)

The evil of silence had taken hold of Jane's soul and much like the broken glass that covered the streets, shards of fear would remain embedded in her for the rest of her life.

"I am so glad that Avi and her family left before all this horror took place," Jane said to herself, and before she turned out the light she said, *"Gute Nacht"* (Good Night) to Max and Moritz as if somehow the little amphibians could pass along her thoughts to her friend that she missed so very much.

But her joy with the frogs would be short lived.

Just four days later Jane walked into her room and discovered both Max and Moritz had died while she was at school. In that shattering moment a voice inside her insisted that it was a sign that Avi was no longer alive either and intuitively she knew it was true.

The thought pushed Jane to her knees and sobbing furiously, she cried out to God praying for her friend Avi, for the little frogs Max & Mortiz, and for all that was changing in her world. So much death, so much destruction, so much that she did not understand.

The loss was incomprehensible.

Part of Jane's heart died along with the little creatures and caused pain so deep that her stomach would hurt for days. But as she was learning, it was best not to talk about any of it.

In the days to follow, she suffered in silence.

CHAPTER EIGHT

Jesus

In the days following Kristallnacht the air was filled with an unholy silence that hung heavy over Germany. The spirit so innate to the Bavarian people, that many fondly called *"Gemuetlichkeit"* (Comfort), was sadly absent. There was a gaping wound in the heart of many as they witnessed their neighbors being forced out quietly, almost unsuspecting of their fate. onto the same streets that Jane and Avi had once played on.

Life continued on as a current of lawlessness and unrest boiled just below the surface. Everyone was compelled to register for a *"Kennkarte"*[5] which was a sheet of thin cardboard, folded in two spots, making it a three-page book. You could not buy food, supplies, ration stamps, or travel without a *Kennkarte*.

---

[5] To receive a Kennkarte (picture ID) an applicant had to fill out an application and provide such documents as birth certificate, pre-war ID, marriage certificate (in specific cases). Upon receiving the card applicants were fingerprinted and a side view photo was taken to show that the ear lobe was not attached to the jaw line as that represented "pure Aryan" heritage.

But life went on and the Raber family adapted.

School was being conducted as close to normal as could have been expected. One day during history class Jane was totally absorbed by the lesson when she heard the sound of footsteps in the hallway. Suddenly, the door opened wide and the entire class jumped in their seats, even the teacher let out an audible gasp.

A difficult looking man with furrowed brow and dark eyes entered the room and securely positioned a ladder by the door. In one swift movement he removed the Crucifix from its longstanding rightful place above the door and replaced it with an image of the Führer.

The sacred space where Jesus Christ once was now held a picture of Adolf Hitler.

Then the man stepped down, wiped his hands as if he had just changed a light bulb, folded up his ladder and walked away leaving a roomful of fourth graders perplexed and con-fused. All eyes turned toward Mrs. Berger, their trusted teacher for answers, but she said nothing. The rest of the day was so very quiet.

It wasn't long before word spread that the growing reach of Hitler's dictatorship included the banning of church publications and removal of cherished and revered religious icons, in order to quell a possible dissent. But in Jane's case, and countless other German children, the die had been cast and the image burned into their young minds. This action taken by the Nazi's was called *"Kirchenkampf."*[6]

When school was let out Jane decided to take a longer route home down Herzog Rudolf street that passed by Avi's school.

There was nothing left but rubble. The school and synagogue were totally destroyed as if a wrecking ball had leveled the structures. Piles of brick and stone stuck out like broken bones, splinters of wood, books, desks, and shattered glass lay in great, gasping heaps.

With tears filling her eyes Jane rushed to get past the

---

[6] *Kirchenkampf (Church struggle) was a region by region attempt to establish authority over the Catholic church and for a time it worked but a conclave of bishops led their people to protest with a degree of effectiveness. Beginning in 1936, Nazis removed crucifixes in schools and the Catholic Bishop of Munster August von Galen protested and public demonstrations followed. In some regions, the images of Hitler were removed, and the Cross of Jesus returned, other regions were left with the Führer above the entry way as a constant reminder of his presence.

carnage and all she could think of was Avi...Frau Steinberger...Black Mari...and even gentle Hedwig. They were
all gone as if they had never been. As she pushed on towards
home she kept repeating the mantra that had reluctantly become a part of her. *"Be strong,"* she admonished herself, *"No
tears, no discussions."*

It was growing dark as Jane approached the stoop in
front of the stone apartment building, so she straightened
up, wiped her cheeks dry, and opened the door to the safest
place on earth.

That night as Jane lay in her bed she prayed hard to
understand the events of the day. She was reassured in the
knowing that while the Nazi's could remove Jesus from her
school room they would never be able to remove him from
her heart.

CHAPTER NINE

Papa

It was a somber gathering on a late November evening in 1938, when Hans Raber assembled his family together in the living room and without any hesitation came right to the point.

"Meine geliebte Familie Wir sind pleite. Bankrott und ohne Mittel der Unterstützung." (My beloved family we are broke. Financially bankrupt and without a means of support.) Hans continued, his voice cracking slightly. *"Niemand kauft Geigen oder nimmt Gitarren Unterricht mehr (*No one is buying violins or guitars or taking lessons anymore*) denn niemand kann sie sich leisten."* (because no one can afford them.) Hans composed himself for a moment, put a finger on his chin and said, *"Aber wir sind nicht allein, ganz Deutschland ist in einer wirtschaftlichen Depression."* (But we are not alone my family, the whole of Germany is in an economic depression.)

Mama, of course, knew what her husband was going to say, but hearing the words come out of his mouth was quite another thing. She looked at Nocki, Karl, and Jane with a longing gaze as they sat silently listening to their father speak.

Sensing his children's growing discomfort, Hans lifted his head a bit higher, folded his hands across his chest, and spoke in a firm tone, *"Jedoch, es ist ein Strahl der Hoffnung! Ich habe eine Stelle als Kapellmeister an der Oper in Halle an der Saale bekommen!"* (However, there is a ray of hope! I have been offered a position as conductor at the opera in Halle on Saale!) He tried very hard to sound certain in the midst of such uncertainty.

The children's faces mirrored both surprise and perplexity, and before any of them could digest his words and ask what it all meant Mama spoke up.

"Ja, es ist wahr Kinder, euer Vater muss morgen schon mit dem Zug früh weg sein Engagement in Halle fängt sofort an und ist für zwei Saisonen festgelegt." (It's a fact children, your father is leaving on the train tomorrow. His engagement in Halle starts immediately and will last for two seasons.) She quickly ended the discussion with a firm but loving, *"Jetzt macht euch bereit fürs Bett Kinder, und vergesst nicht euere*

Gebete zu sagen." (Now get ready for bed, Children, and don't forget to say your prayers.)

Nocki, Karl, and Jane bid their parents good night. A short time later Jane lay in her bed, her mind swirling with all that had taken place in just one day. Her beloved Jesus been removed and replaced by the Führer. It was Hitler who had promised so much to the people of Germany and now the country was in a depression. Wasn't it his fault that people were unable to afford violins forcing Papa to leave his family and seek work in Halle that was 300 miles away?

"Oh Papa, I will miss you so," Jane cried into her pillow. When her tears subsided, she closed her eyes, clasped her hands in prayer and said, *"Gott ist mein Erhalter und Kompass"* (God is my sustainer and compass) and then she recalled the words to her favorite verse in Romans 8:28 and whispered them into the darkness… *"Und wir wissen, dass alle Dinge zum Guten mitwirken, denen, die Gott lieben, die berufen sind nach seinem Vorsatz."* (And we know that in all things God works for the good of those who love him, who have been called according to his purpose.)

She would need all her strength to say goodbye to Papa

in the morning. After a time, she let the day go behind her and drifted off to sleep.

The next day was full of both excitement and sadness as Mama and the children had to bid their beloved husband and father goodbye at the *München Hauptbahnhof.* (Munich main train station.)

The boys' attention was drawn to the hustle and bustle of people and trains that were scattered on a myriad of tracks, departing and arriving at their exact appointed times.

"Papa, will you come back soon?" pleaded Jane, pulling on the sleeve of her father's heavy overcoat.

Seeing tears well up in his daughter's eyes he quickly answered, "Ja, Janerl, just as soon as I get my first break I will come back to you all."

As his words spilled out Hans could feel his own eyes filling with tears and hoping to avoid them rolling down his face, he quickly turned to Karl and said, "Well my son, seeing as you are now eleven and as the oldest you are going to be the man of the house for a while. That entitles you to take your mother, brother, and sister to the nearest *Eisdiele* (ice cream parlor) for some ice cream," as he handed him a few coins.

An ear to ear grin broke across Karl's face. "I'm the man of the house," he repeated out loud so both eight-year-old Nocki and ten-year-old Jane could hear. Turning back to his father he said, "Yes, Papa, I will watch over them."

Hans Raber pulled his family close, not wanting to let them go, he was grateful for the opportunity to work at his craft and earn money to take care of his family, even though they would be so very far apart.

There they stood, as the trains bleated out their warnings, horns cutting through the late fall day making the air feel even colder.

Finally, he stepped onto the train that would take him to Halle on Saale and the position of conductor at the opera. As the train began to pull away, he glanced back at his most treasured possessions waving at him from the platform. In that holy moment, unbeknownst to him, it would be the last time he and his beloved family would ever see each other.

Just three weeks later, Jane returned home from school to horrible news. Mama had received a telegram earlier that morning informing her that during an incredible performance of Giuseppe Verdi's "Aida" Papa suffered a massive heart attack that instantly claimed his life.

Upon hearing of her father's death, it tore apart the few remaining pieces of Jane's heart that still contained light. The world would become an even darker place now that her beloved Papa would never again walk in the door, lift her up and say *"Grüess Gott Janerl"* while she giggled and dug in his coat pockets for a hidden bit of candy.

Jane knew her Mama had just lost her beloved Hans, but as was her way, she made her thoughts known to her children in no uncertain terms. With her arms folded across her chest and in stern but loving way she spoke, *"Kinder, ich habe mich schon alleine ausgeweint aber ich weiss, ihr braucht ebenfalls Zeit um über euren Vater zu trauern."* (Children, I did my crying. You must have your time to cry as well for Papa.) *"Ich aber muss nun über unsere Zukunft studieren wie unser Leben weitergehen soll."* (But I have to sort out how I am going to make a living for us. With God's help I will find a way.) As the years went on, she would do just that.

An incredible and gentle man, who had carried on his father's legacy and filled the world with music, the dignified, proud, and steady influence in the family, Hans Raber was only 47 years old when he died.

CHAPTER TEN

Bombs

It was a beautiful crisp fall morning that ushered in the first day of September 1939.

Newspapers and radios announced that Germany had invaded Poland[7] and the propaganda speeches that followed predicted how Germany was going to dominate the entire world. A palpable sense of national pride was emanating from the general populace and with it a heightened sense of confidence in Adolf Hitler.

Jane and her new friend from the apartment building down the block, Gretchen Koenig, often walked to school together and this morning was no different, even though the air felt much heavier than usual.

"*Grüess Gott,* Jane," said Gretchen.

"*Grüess Gott,* Gretchen."

---

[7] In January 1934 Germany signed a non-aggression pact with Poland, which disrupted the French network of anti-German alliances in Eastern Europe. In March 1939, Hitler demanded the return of the Free City of Danzig and the Polish Corridor, a strip of land that separated East Prussia from the rest of Germany. The British announced they would come to the aid of Poland if it was attacked. Hitler, believing the British would not actually take action, ordered an invasion plan should be readied for a target date of September 1939.

The usual carefree girl chatter that occupied their walk most mornings was absent, both girls deep in their own thoughts just continued on their familiar fifteen-minute walk to school in silence.

They arrived just as the school bell rang, and found their seats in a hushed classroom filled with great expectation of what this most unusual and fearful day might bring.

The teacher, Miss Gerabach, rapped on her heavy desk to get the attention of the class even though the room was already dead silent.

She heaved up a large box from the floor beside her desk and then spilled the contents out for all to see.

A chorus of gasps emanated from the students along with whispers of "gas masks."

Miss Gerabach steadied herself, went to the blackboard, and with the chalk screeching a bit on the slate, wrote a sinister looking word in large bold letters.

HEXAMETHELENTETRAMIN.

"Class, your very important assignment today is to study this word and remember it well. It's the word for one of the many poisonous gases that were used in World War I from 1914 to

1918. This gas might once again be used as we are now engaged in another war." Miss Gerabach's words to a roomful of young children was not just a warning but also a command. She knew that their lives and the lives of their families and friends might depend on her instructions.

Jane sat and wondered about where all this was going. Papa was no longer alive to calm her fears, and while she really enjoyed her friendship with Gretchen, she missed Avi so very much. Every day it seemed the newspapers and radio flooded the people with messages that seemed very hopeful but underneath it all there was a sense of dread as well.

The rest of the day in school was filled with training exercises on how to properly put on a gas mask and make sure that it fit just right.

Drills were held that included making practice runs to the basement while the alarm system in the school sounded its warning.

But through all the day, Jane did the one thing that above all else had become most important in her life.

She prayed.

She would need those prayers as the next four years

would bring with it untold hardships, food became very scarce and hunger became rampant. If one had anything of value at all it became a bargaining tool on the thriving black market. All sorts of items ranging from jewelry to family heirlooms became a way to secure food. A winter hat might buy a spoon of pig's fat or the luxury of butter. A trinket could buy a rabbit (but it could also be a wayward cat that when skinned resembled a rabbit.)

The abundance of the past was rapidly becoming nothing more than a lingering memory.

By 1943, the preparation Miss Gerabach had given the class back in 1939 was of no use, as the warfare was made of fire, not gas. Bombs rained down on the cities at night, shaking the earth with their thunder and causing massive destruction.

Over time the bombings ramped up and the giant metal monsters dropped from the sky, scattering people who sought refuge from the onslaught and since there was no radar in Germany, sometimes there was no warning of the deluge until it was too late.

One of the most shocking sights Jane beheld came one

cold winter morning as she and Gretchen were confronted with the shattered image of their school reduced to rubble. The girls stood there in shock, as there was nothing left of *Del Vechci Private School for Girls*, but a smoldering heap of concrete, twisted steel, and broken dreams. To Jane, the destruction was eerily similar to Avi's school just a few years earlier.

The school president, Professor Aldus Del Vechci was perched atop the fallen ruins looking scattered and distant, his usual staid demeanor shaken to the core. He informed the students as they arrived that the school would continue on once a new location was found. They were to return home and watch the mail for the announcement as to where and when they could report to school once again.

Jane and Gretchen walked home in silence, which was sadly becoming normal.

Instead of heading straight into her house, Jane sat for a few moments outside the movie theater next door and re-peated her prayers for strength through this very difficult time, reaching out to God for answers to questions she didn't understand at all.

When Mama heard about the bombing of the school she collapsed onto a kitchen chair.

Seeing her mother's distress, Jane boldly proclaimed "Mama, I'll quit school. I can help. Nocki is still in public school and Karl is in the Navy. You need me here now."

In a determined voice Mama said, "Jane, you are only fifteen years old and I will not hear of you quitting school. With God's help, we will make out fine. While I have no particular skills, I'm planning on another job as a *Hausmeisterin* (housekeeper) at that large apartment building at Thiersch Street." Jane started to object to Mama taking on another job, but Mama continued, "Yes, I know it means scrubbing down the stairs and bannisters, but the extra income will help us make it. Besides, I can sublet our two big bedrooms."

"Don't worry Janerl," she said, using Papa's treasured nickname for Jane, "Don't worry."

Three weeks after the bombing, Jane and Gretchen were excited to join a group of "Del Vechci Girls" at the München Hauptbahnhof getting ready to board a train to Garmisch/Partenkirchen and then on to their new home at Castle Waldkrone, situated on the summit of a widespread plateau within the safety of the majestic Bavarian Alps.

"Have you ever lived in a castle before?" Lisi asked as the group began its one hour climb up the steep, tree lined mountain pass to Castle Waldkrone.

"Oh no, I have never lived in a castle," replied Heidi, "but my brother and I visited King Ludwig's castle, Schloss Linderhof, with all its regal splendor and its gilded rooms." Then with a hint of sadness in her voice, she added, "But that was before it was closed, because of the war."

The girls made their way up the mountain, walking in silence as each of them had thoughts of their homes that were fading behind them with each passing step. The stillness and serenity of the glorious Alps was in sharp contrast to war torn Munich where sirens, bombings and the devastation of war prevailed.

As Jane walked in wonderment of nature, she felt much closer to God, up so high above the chaos that she had lived in for a very long time. While unsure of the steps that needed to be taken, she was sure that God would guide her way but her thoughts were interrupted when suddenly Heidi blurted out, "LOOK! THERE IT IS!

This outburst caused the line of young girls to stop in their tracks and look up in awe of the sight that loomed before them, the place that would become both school, sanctuary and home, the safe haven of Castle Waldkrone.

CHAPTER ELEVEN

The Castle

"Sign in and fill out this sheet of paper," ordered Fraülein Sabine, the school's secretary, to the eager students who began to pass through the massive ornate double doors that led into the foyer of the castle. "Every one of you must fill out this form," she snapped again, making sure that she was heard by all. Miss Sabine, as the students would come to call her, was a stern but loving presence, just the thing that was needed for a war-weary group of young minds.

Jane stepped up to a large table with her paper.

"This is your room number. It's in the west wing," Miss Sabine said. "Just follow the signs," she added. Jane took a few steps into the large vestibule and stopped for a moment to let her eyes fully absorb the enormously high ceiling with its equally long brocade drapes that framed the clear glass windows. The half-moon shaped staircase in the center beckoned from another time, of riches, opulence, refinement, and majesty.

After seeing so much destruction, Jane stood in awe of the beauty that surrounded her and it took a moment or two for it all to sink in.

"Papa would love this," she thought to herself.

Jane found her way to the west wing of the castle and ultimately to room Number 60. She took a deep breath, opened the door and before she could introduce herself she heard, "Don't put your suitcase on my bed, this lower bunk is mine," said a dark-haired girl, obviously pointing the words in Jane's direction. "You can have the upper bunk."

Jane stood for a moment not quite sure what to do.

"C'mon in, I'm Edith," said a pretty blonde curly haired girl from the other lower bunk across the room. "That's Marianne, don't mind her. You'll get used to her bossy ways if you just take what she says as entertainment and nothing else."

Marianne scowled a bit in defiance of Edith's words, as Jane walked over to the upper bunk above Marianne's and heaved her suitcase onto the small bed. The girls made further introductions and wondered who would be next to occupy the last bunk above Ellie's when the door opened wide and Gretchen walked in.

"My, I am so very glad to see you," said Jane with a sigh of relief at the sight of her friend. "Did you hear Miss Sabine making a strict rule against allowing close friends to be in the same room? Something to do with fraternizing being a deterrent to good study habits."

"Well, no one has to know do they Jane?" Gretchen smiled.

"Well, they don't have to worry about me," Marianne announced. "I don't like to be pals with anyone. And, just get a load of these straw-packed mattresses," she sniffed. "Hmm…some castle."

By the evening of the first day most of the 250 students were settled in their respective rooms and now as it was nearing supper time, they began to gradually make their descent down the regal, half-moon shaped staircase, and congregate in front of the dining room.

The nervous conversation created a palpable buzz, but all went silent as the doors opened promptly at six o'clock sharp revealing five long tables with chairs on both sides and steaming hot plates of food. They were filled with mashed potatoes, apple sauce, five crunchy beautiful red radishes, a thick slice of crusty dark bread, and a tall glass of milk topped off the fare. To the hungry young students, it looked like a meal fit for royalty.

The chairs quickly filled up and the students gulped down the food as it had never been there in the first place. Not a single scrap was left over, every plate was clean.

After supper, it wasn't long before Jane and Gretchen took off to explore every nook and cranny of the castle.

The east and west wings housed the dorms. The south wing was reserved for faculty members and was off limits to students unless by personal invite. The kitchen was situated just off the vestibule next to the faculty quarters.

Feeling full from dinner and safe at her new home Jane stepped into the kitchen and noticing the massive iron cooking stove she got an idea and made her way to it. "What are you doing?" Gretchen whispered loudly, afraid someone would find them. Her curiosity was aroused as she watched Jane leaning over the stove, stretching to reach the flue to open it.

"I'm scraping off some of the soot from the flue onto this piece of white paper," Jane answered incredulously, as if Gretchen should know the procedure.

"What for?" said Gretchen with puzzled look.

"You'll see," Jane replied, a slight smile on her face.

Back in their room, Jane busied herself making a paste mixing castor oil with the soot from the kitchen and then dipped a small brush into the concoction and began to apply it to her eye lashes.

A few moments later, she turned her face to her room-mates, batted her eyes like a movie star and said, "Well, what do you think? Zarah Leander or Marlene Dietrich?"

"Neither," the girls giggled in unison. "Ha, just look at yourself with all those black dots around your eyes from blinking," they laughed.

"You look like Frankenstein's next of kin," chided Marianne. "Oh, you are just jealous," Jane shot back. "I'm going to put on some lipstick."

"Lipstick? Where can you get lipstick?" Marianne scoffed. "That luxury has been out of circulation since the war began," she insisted.

"Ah," said Jane. "But I have some red shoe polish that will do the trick and works just as well."

The four girls enjoyed a few moments of frivolity with the "make up" and suddenly the war seemed very far away.

Then came a knock at the door.

It was Miss Sabine carrying a tray with four cups and a teapot filled with hot peppermint tea and a large pretzel that had been cut into four pieces. You could have heard a pin drop when she entered the room. One look at the girls and a very stern look came over her face.

Letting out a heavy sigh Miss Sabine said, "This kind of behavior cannot and will not be tolerated in any way."

The girls looked at her with blank stares of innocence even with their faces looking a bit like connect-a-dots puzzles of black and red.

The woman surveyed her charges, composed herself and continued.

"Since this is obviously your first offense, I will let it rest. But that's it, no more of this foolishness."

The girls shook their heads in agreement, Miss Sabine put the tray down and left the room. When the girls felt it was safe, they giggled again and were grateful for the tea, a tasty pretzel, and each other.

Although intense study was the order of the day, it was always mingled in with concern and anxiety over the bombings that continued and the welfare of their families back home. Every day at lunchtime came a 30-minute news broadcast that was turned on for the benefit of the students to hear the latest updates. In the evening, just after supper, another half hour of news brought the war home to the students behind the massive stone walls of Waldkrone Castle.

Two years passed quickly for Jane and her roommates.

It was 1945 and U.S. troops were only days, if not hours, outside of Munich. Hitler and his Nazi regime were being toppled and World War II was nearly over.

Despite the news, Professor Aldus Del Vechci kept a tight pace on meeting an early deadline of April 27th for the big day of graduation instead of the original date of May 22nd.

When the day finally arrived, smiling faces were to be seen in every corner of the castle as young ladies of seventeen and eighteen years of age walked out of the superintendent's office, waving their newly acquired diploma, The Abitur.

The words of Professor Del Vechci echoed in their ears as they celebrated their achievements. "Ladies, rumor has it that some of you are ready to up and leave. I understand you are anxious about your family and friends back home and would like to leave right now," he announced. "I cannot hold you back from doing so. However, I strongly urge you not to leave just yet, but to stay here under my protection until such a time as is deemed safe to return home.

Jane heard his words but was silently making other plans.

She had been away from Mama and home for so long, worried so very much and prayed harder than she had ever done before. Despite what she might encounter outside the walls of Castle Waldkrone, *she knew* that God would protect her on the journey back to Munich come what may.

She had entered the castle as a frightened girl and was ready to leave as a vibrant, educated young woman.

It was time to make her way back home, no matter what.

CHAPTER TWELVE

The Train

Jane was busy stuffing her belongings into a little suitcase when Gretchen came into the room.

"What are you doing? Are you leaving?" Gretchen exclaimed.

"Yes, I am. I can no longer stand not knowing what is happening at home Gretchen. I just heard on the radio that there was a fierce bombing last night that left 127 dead. I don't even know if my house is still standing and if Mama is okay."

Gretchen watched her friend closely as she spoke, realizing there would be no talking Jane out of leaving, despite what Professor Del Vechci had insisted would be a dangerous, possibly fatal decision.

"Wait Jane, I'm going with you," Gretchen finally announced. "I'm going, too."

Jane glanced at her friend. It would be good to have her along, but she also sensed that both of them could be heading into serious trouble. It was one thing for her to make the choice to leave, but quite another thing for Gretchen to follow. Neither girl thought far enough ahead to consider the danger that might lie before them. Once Gretchen had stowed her belongings they stepped towards the door of the room but then Jane stopped just short of leaving and said, "We must pray for a safe trip home, Gretchen. We must ask God to guide our way."

Gretchen nodded in agreement, the two girls bowed their heads, folded their hands, and then Jane spoke in a whisper asking God to grant guidance and safe passage on their way home.

The girls hugged each other, squared their shoulders and began to make their way out of the safety of Castle Waldkrone, but not before making a quick stop by the kitchen.

There was the school cook, Kuni, busy preparing what appeared to be asparagus soup for the evening meal. She was so involved in her preparations, at first, she didn't even notice the girls until Gretchen cleared her throat loudly, which startled Kuni.

"Well hello, girls, what can I get you? Or perhaps you just want to help old Kuni scrub some sooty pots and pans?"

She laughed out loud, as was her way. Over time all the girls in the castle had become very fond of the woman who prepared all their meals and who had a sympathetic ear and warm heart. But Kuni could tell that something was amiss.

"What is it, girls? What do you need?"

Jane tilted her head up high and spoke in a tone she hoped would sound much stronger than she was actually feeling in that moment. "We have decided to go home, Kuni. We need food for our journey back to Munich,"

Kuni put her hands on her hips and realized that there would be no persuading the girls to stay so she wiped her hands on her apron and softly said, "Come with me to the pantry."

Kuni opened the pantry door to reveal a couple of onions and five boiled potatoes. "This is what we have left today," said Kuni with a look of disgust on her weathered face.

After a short discussion, Jane and Gretchen decided to take just two boiled potatoes, one for each of them. "Not much, but it will have to do," said Jane. They both hugged Kuni, took one last look around the sanctuary they had spent so many days in and then Jane declared, "It's now or never Gretchen. Let's go."

The trek from Castle Waldkrone to the village of Waldblick took just about a half hour down a zig-zag path through the forest. As the stone walls of the castle quickly faded behind them in the distance Jane and Gretchen made it just in time to board the last train of the day headed for Munich.

The girls remained mostly silent on the ride because conversation would have been near impossible as the old iron relic of a train screeched so loudly along the tracks that it was deafening to the ears. For five long hours they bumped and clanked along the rails until at last the train came to a shuddering halt. The girls looked out the windows and watched passengers scattering in all directions as the conductor bellowed through a hand-held bullhorn, *"Alles aussteigen! Der Zug geht nicht mehr weiter. Alliierte Truppen sind sehr nahe bei München und nähern sich von allen Seiten! Alles ist eingestellet. Es gibt keine Zeitungen und keinen Rundfunk! Alles sofort aussteigen!"* (Everybody off the train! This is as far as we go! Foreign troops are very close to Munich and are

approaching from all sides! There are no newspapers and radio stations have stopped broadcasting!*) "Alles muss raus!"*
(Leave the train now!)

The conductor started to repeat his message, but Jane
and Gretchen didn't stick around to hear it twice. They fled
the train and joined the throng of people walking toward Munich.

After a short while of pushing through unfamiliar and
treacherous terrain Jane shouted, "Gretchen! Stop! I have
such a pain in my side from all this running!"

Gretchen looked back at her friend, now doubled over
in pain and nodded her head. They stood for a few minutes,
huffing and puffing to catch their breath among the bombed-
out ruins of buildings when suddenly both girls said the same
thing at the very same time, "Do you know where we are?"
They each let out a short laugh at the shared thought. "I think
so. The train had stopped somewhere way past Freising,"
Jane offered hopefully.

"Yes, and it's still quite some ways to walk before we
get to Munich," said Gretchen. "Jane?" she continued.

"Yes, Gretchen?"

"I'm really scared. It's starting to get dark now and there is not a single soul in sight, we don't really know where we are, this is just an empty country road with bombed out houses," said Gretchen as she waived her hands at the destruction all around them.

In order to quell her own fear Jane replied, "I have an idea, let's go into that bombed out ruin over there and see if we can find a place to rest for bit and get off this road."

Gretchen needed no further prodding and the girls took off into a soft run and found a small alcove amid the ruins that would at least offer some shelter from the elements and out of sight from any possible strangers on the road.

They spread out their blankets and put down their small suitcases to use as pillows as exhaustion pushed them to the ground and staring into the quickening darkness.
The hunger pangs in their bellies made loud sounds and they quickly consumed the two cold, boiled potatoes that tasted so good. They relished each and every bite.

In the distance muffled sounds of artillery fire made the ground tremble and occasionally the sky would light up as an explosion would erupt.

The warmth and protection of Castle Waldkrone was quickly becoming a distant memory.

The girls huddled together a bit for warmth against the cold night air, and whispered to each other, "*pray*."

Quietly, with the sounds of war as their backdrop Jane and Gretchen each spoke to their Lord Jesus for courage, protection, and safety for themselves and their families.

The morning had begun with such conviction at the castle. The decision to leave, the kindly look on Kuni's face, seeing homes destroyed where families once lived, and the very real ache of their feet were all part of one of the most difficult days of their young lives.

Then, totally spent from the long day, they drifted off into a quasi-restful sleep such as only the very young could possibly muster up under the circumstances.

Tomorrow was another day.

CHAPTER THIRTEEN

Home

The early morning sun was breaking across the war-torn landscape, shining through the trees. A few strands of light were beginning to illuminate the little hideout in the ruins.

But it was the sound of distant guns that woke Gretchen first.

"Jane, wake up, it's nearly daylight. We have to start moving again. C'mon, let's go, I'll take the blankets, you take the suitcases" she said.

Jane woke up at the sound of her friend's voice, rubbed her eyes, and nodded in agreement.

Minutes later they resumed their trek. As their steps quickened, they could see a weather-beaten object in the distance. As they got closer, they recognized that it was a worn and windblown waiting station for tram passengers going to Munich.

"Gretchen, look. The sign says Nymphenburg, that means we are only one or two kilometers outside of Munich."

The sound of gunfire had grown closer as well,

confirming the girls were getting nearer to home.

Encouraged by the sign, they ran a slow but steady pace.

They rounded a curve in the road past a line of shattered trees and ran smack dab into a small fraction of freedom fighters who were manning machine guns and blasting away at an enemy that was within range of their positions.

They were not soldiers, but civilians.

"Keep running Gretchen," puffed Jane, "Look, look this is Maximilianstrasse, we can't stop now, we are so close! We are almost home!"

A few minutes later, the girls could see the old familiar Max II monument in the middle of Maximilianeum Plaza.

They came to an abrupt stop, as if suddenly anchored in their tracks. There in front of them just yards away was a metal beast, a battle-scarred tank, with its muzzle protruding like a giant finger pointed in the direction they were heading.

"Gretchen! I bet it's the Russians! Look, that tank has a five-cornered star on the side!" Jane dropped the suitcases and quickly grabbed a blanket from Gretchen and threw it over their heads. "It's a Russian tank! We must hide our faces, remember what they told us at Waldkrone, that the Russians are rapists!"

The tank began moving very slowly into the circle of Max II plaza when Jane and Gretchen instinctively hit the ground to escape a hail of bullets being fired by snipers from the huge Maximilianeum[8], that sat atop the hill across the River Isar.

They huddled under their blanket, hands clasped in prayer asking God for protection when suddenly…the bullets stopped.

The girls thought it might be safe enough to rise and stand again, but they remained under the "protection" of their blanket.

When they dared to peek around they saw an unbeliev-able sight. There was a small band of ten or eleven-year-old boys in their Hitler Youth uniforms with their HJ knives strapped into a sheath on their small waists.
They were just children, in the midst of a full-blown combat zone.

---

[8] The Maximilianeum, is a palatial building in Munich, that was built as the home of a gifted students' foundation.

This little band of would be defenders was led by a very old man sporting a leather helmet, the kind worn by WWI Messerschmitt pilots. He was also lugging a heavy *"Panzerfaust"* or anti-tank weapon under his arm with some difficulty.

Suddenly, the lid atop the tank popped open and a uniformed soldier appeared with weapon in hand.

"Oh no, they are going to shoot that old man and those boys," Gretchen wailed.

The solider excavated himself from the tank, looked sternly at the old man as he walked towards him and in one movement put an arm around the old man's shoulder and in a commanding tone said, "Give me that, Pop. We don't want anyone to get hurt here."

The grizzled old man blinked a couple of times, looked at his ragged band of boys and said, *"Ich muss mein Vaterland verteidigen."* (I must protect my fatherland.)

"Yeah, Pop, I know," the soldier said as he gently took the Panzerfaust from him and handed it to another soldier. "Now take those boys and get out of here," he said, motioning in the opposite direction for effect.

"GRETCHEN, DID YOU HEAR THEM SPEAK?" Jane blurted.

"YES, I DID," she said with joy in her voice. They looked at each other and blurted out, "THEY ARE AMERICANS!"

The girls flung their "protection blanket" unceremoniously to the ground. "No need for this now," said Jane, "at least we know they are not Russians."

The little band of boys and the old man left quietly, a look back at the Maximilianeum revealed that the snipers, two German officers in their black SS uniforms, were being taken away by American GI's and forced into an open Jeep.

The girls surveyed the situation, paused for a moment looked each other in the eyes, and while holding hands they realized they were alive.

Jane spoke for both of them when she said, "C'mon, Gretchen, let's go home. I think the war is over."

They bolted the short distance towards the corner that turned onto their street. What they saw shocked them. They spotted Jane's house first.

It was unharmed.

But the building next door, the old movie theater was gone, gutted and burned to the ground.

Then Gretchen broke into a dead run up the two blocks where her home was and suddenly she came to an abrupt halt. Gretchen stood frozen, staring at what used to be her house. There was nothing left. It lay in total ruin, a bombed-out shell.

Jane rushed to her friend's side and tried to console her as best she could, but Gretchen was shaking so hard Jane had a hard time holding on to her. They slowly walked back towards Jane's house. The two of them had come so far and now this.

Gretchen, in shock and disbelief, kept mumbling over and over again, *"Wo ist meine Mutter? Wo ist meine Mutter?"* (Where is my mother? Where is my mother?)

Unbeknownst to the girls in that moment, on the night of April 29th, just two days after the girls had received their diplomas at Waldkrone, Munich was bombed once again and Gretchen's mother, Zenta, survived by taking shelter in a common underground bunker. When she climbed out of the bunker she came face to face with the fact that her life was literally in ruins. The Allied bombs had erased all physical reminders of the life she held near and dear to her heart.

Her husband was killed at the Russian front a year earlier, now her home a smoldering heap of memories, and she had no idea if Gretchen was dead or alive, it felt like everything worth living for was gone.

Zenta wandered aimlessly that horrible night for a very long time, in a daze of sorts, the reality of the situation not sinking into her mind. Under skies still ablaze from the aftermath of firebombs, she found herself in front of Jane's house that was beyond all odds, still intact.

Karola had opened her door to find Zenta standing there mute and shell shocked. Her heart went out to her friend and neighbor, and she pulled her in to safety...

Jane was heartbroken for her friend and said, "Gretchen lets go back to my house. Maybe Mama will know where your mother is." Holding Gretchen close to her, Jane led her back down the street. When Karola answered her doorbell, a great reunion took place. The girls were finally reunited with their mothers, tears of joy, hugs of happiness, and prayers of thanksgiving were shared. The destruction of Munich seemed very far away, even though they were standing in the middle of it all.

CHAPTER FOURTEEN

America

Three years had passed since World War II ended and with Adolph Hitler gone the world had started to put the puzzle pieces of humanity back in place. Not long after the war ended Gretchen met a young GI that she fancied, and he had a friend, a tall, handsome man named Maxwell Horton, a U.S. Air Force Cpl.

Jane and Max met, fell in love, and by August 1948 Jane Raber had become Mrs. Jane Horten, the wife of U.S. Air Force Cpl. Maxwell Horten. But now it was October and she was sitting onboard a giant C-47 airship. This mighty airship that had once carried troops and war machines to Europe had been refitted as a transport for about fifty or so new "war brides."[9] Jane smiled to herself as she watched the crew

---

[9] War bride is a term used in reference to foreign women who married military personnel in times of war or during their military occupations of foreign countries, especially–but not exclusively–during World War I and World War II. One of the largest and best documented war bride phenomena is American servicemen marrying German "Fräuleins" after World War II. By 1949, over 20,000 German war brides had emigrated to the United States.

getting ready to serve lunch and thought, "That in and of itself is so very American."

Now for the first time she was about to land on U.S. soil at LaGuardia Airport, her feet finally touching this immense land of freedom and endless opportunity that she had only read about in books.

A great fan of the German author Karl May, his novels like *Old Shatterhand* and *Winnetou* were set against the backdrop of the American Old West. These books were very popular with all the kids in Germany who virtually devoured them as soon they were available and passed around many times at school.

Looking out the window with New York in the distance, she reminded herself that it was Delaware, not the rugged Old West, that would be her destination. Try as she may to focus, Jane's mind was racing from one subject to another. Her excitement was in high gear. She was going to live in America.

THE UNITED STATES OF AMERICA! The mere thought that she was going to begin a new chapter in such an incredible place was almost too much to bear. What would it be like? How would people respond to her as a German? The truth was that she, along with all the other brides on the plane, were still considered "enemies" until a very special and coveted document was completed, signed, and she officially became a U.S. citizen.

Jane settled back in her seat, content in the knowing that God had taken her this far and, while it might not be easy, her faith would see her through. She took a deep breath and began to read a copy of the United States Constitution, which had been handed out to everyone on the plane.

Max was to be discharged from the military soon and, in the meantime, she was to meet his family at Camp Kilmer in New Jersey. They would then take Jane to their home in Delaware where she would reunite with her tall, blond, and very handsome husband.

The bus ride through New York City was nearly beyond her comprehension. All those giant buildings, their windows ablaze with bright lights making it look like daylight even though it was three o'clock in the morning! Through the bus window she watched the sidewalks and storefronts zip by as the bus wheeled its way through the "Big

Apple." At a stoplight Jane caught a glimpse of a man dressed in a black business suit and hat casually reading a newspaper. This was quite a contrast from Munich, where everything was under a "black out" and curfew began after sundown.

Finally, the bus pulled into Camp Kilmer. Jane's new in-laws had been eagerly awaiting her arrival. It was a heaven-sent moment for sure, awkward in some ways, and yet somehow Jane knew that God had played a role in all of it.

The years that followed her first steps in America were filled with amazing, unique experiences. Getting to know her new home and surroundings, her new in-laws and, of course, her new husband Max.

All of it, the good and the bad, the challenging times, and beautiful ones felt blessed from on high…full of providence and purpose.

The most glorious moment of all came in 1949 when she first held her newborn son Eddie and the subsequent joy of watching him grow into a wonderful young man. Eddie was a good boy who was always at his mother side and wanted to be part of all that was going on, eager to help as needed…even if it meant operating on a chicken.

One bright day in 1954 Max walked in the back door of their suburban two-story home after a long day of work as a pipefitter for B&O Railroad.

"Jane," he called out, "Grandma Wisser wants you to come over and talk with her about a problem she has with one of her chickens."

That brought Jane into the room very fast. "Me?" she asked. "I don't know anything about chickens, Max, I'm a big city girl, remember?"

Max just gave Jane a nod and wink. She quickly went next door, knocked and let herself in.

"Well," said Grandma Wisser, in her West Virginia drawl. "I just don't know what to do with this little ole chicken, Jane. It was the runt of the litter and them two hundred other chickens won't let it get near enough to the food trough to feed. The poor little critter has gotta forage on that stringy onion grass growing around the yard and its craw is getting' bigger and bigger and its little body is getting' weaker and weaker. Pretty soon it's gonna die," anguished

Grandma Wisser.

"Wish there was some way to save it…Jane, can you think of anything?"

Jane thought for a moment or two about the dilemma of the little bird and announced, "Well Grandma, I'll just have to open it up and clean out it's craw," she said. "Can't promise anything but maybe it will help."

Jane flew into action and wasted no time getting everything ready for the "surgery" that would be performed on a wooden make-shift table in the hen house.

The *"scalpel"* was a razor blade, the *"sutures"* common needle and thread, and for a *"sponge"* a few clean rags with water along with the *"anesthetic"* which was chloroform.

Just five years old at the time, Eddie stood by his mother ready to assist with the procedure, but first Jane gave him some instructions.

"Keep your nose turned away as much as you can so you won't breathe in any of the fumes from the chloroform, but you have to also keep an eye on the chicken for any movement it might make that would mean it was waking up.

If it moves put another drop of chloroform on the cotton pad on its beak."

Eddie was steadfast in his duties and Jane was able to clean out the craw of the bird and stitch it back up. Grandma was so happy at the outcome and when it came time to sell the little bird she spared its life, named it "*Clucker*" and it became her pet.

It was during this time, as a busy young wife and mother, that a door opened up and Jane's faith would be transformed.

Oral Roberts, the Christian Evangelist, was holding a prayer meeting not far from where Max and Jane lived. They decided to attend and listen to the charismatic preacher who was bringing his healing ministry to the masses. His message of Pentecostalism carried with it something that Jane had been seeking her whole life, almost without knowing it.

A personal relationship with Jesus Christ.

Raised as a Lutheran, Jane had been taught that God was "*out there*" but listening to the powerful words of Oral Roberts it was revealed to her that in fact The Holy Spirit resided "*within her*" and she knew that the time had come for her to be "born again." Jane waited in a long line of people during this healing ministry and was slapped on the forehead by the preacher when it was her turn. Interestingly enough, a bothersome rash she had for some time, soon disappeared.

Her "new commitment" began to help ease the horrors of the war, erasing the stains left on her soul by the memories of Kristallnacht, the deaths of both Avi and Papa, the time Jesus had been replaced with Hitler in school, and a thousand other shards of pain inflicted during the war years.

This was a time of rebirth for Jane, a glorious reckoning of spirit and wholeness, a renewed sense of peace and purpose came upon her.

It was a greater dimension of faith that she had never experienced before, and it brought with it a strength that she would need, for there were more changes and challenges that awaited her in the years to come.

CHAPTER FIFTEEN

Vietnam

The calendar on the wall proclaimed "1960." It was the year that John F. Kennedy would win the Presidential election, NASA launched the Pioneer 5 space probe, and the United States announced that it was sending 3,500 "military advisors" to a far-off land called Vietnam.

Twelve years had passed since Jane had left Germany to begin her new life. Much had transpired in that time. Her marriage to Max was a blessing - a wonderful benefit of the war ending. Her son Eddie was growing strong and tall like his father and was by all accounts an "All-American Boy," which gave Jane great pride.

It would also be the year that Jane's mother would come to live with the family in Delaware. The years after WWII had been difficult ones in Germany. Karola made a living by working for others, taking in sewing, and cleaning duties. She had buried her beloved Nocki when he passed away from a congenital heart defect at the age of 24 but was home to greet Karl after his time in the Navy when the war ended. They lived together, as they once did, but in time she decided to sell everything she could, left Karl to take care of the house, and make her way to Jane.

It was a joyful reunion, but Jane's happiness was short lived. Max had contracted a bacterial infection known as Legionnaire's Disease and Jane's world came crashing down when Max, after valiant battle, died in 1961.

The loss was beyond comprehension and was especially hard on thirteen-year-old Eddie, who adored his father so very much. Jane's world was once again turned upside down, and inside out. The man who had brought her to America, the love of her life was gone.

She was now the breadwinner for Mama Raber and Eddie, who was glad he had his grandmother by his side during such a difficult time. Jane found employment at the local Blue Cross & Blue Shield insurance company to earn her way in the world as a single mom. Together, the three of them moved forward despite the difficulties and challenges that had been thrust upon them.

But there was a bright spot.

At a chance meeting in 1966 at a ski club, Chris Johnson, a United States Air Force Captain, navigated his way into Jane's path. He was square jawed and blond with an air of confidence that comes from military bearing and a deep sense of self-esteem. They connected immediately and grew closer over time. Chris was headquartered at Dover AFB and serving in Africa and he would come and go to the United States seeing Jane as his schedule would allow.

For Jane, meeting Chris was a burst of light in a world that had been dark for some time, and he would be the man to illuminate her heart once again. Jane maintained correspondence with Chris which strengthened her, but also made her heart ache since he was so far away.

As Jane's relationship with Chris grew, she had no idea her relationship with Eddie would be changing. Shortly after graduating from high school in 1967 and in a "love of country, patriotic moment," Eddie stopped at a recruiting office and pledged his young life to the United States Marine Corps.

When her seventeen-year old son opened the front door and proudly proclaimed, "Mom! I'm a Marine!" Jane could hardly believe his words.

Aghast, Jane cried out, "That can't be! You're not old enough, you are just a boy!" Memories of young men going off to battle and not returning flooded her mind.

Eddie stuck out his chest with great pride and said, "Marines build men and that is what I want to be!"

She knew there was no talking him out of it, he had to do what he felt he needed to do. The number of American soldiers in Vietnam had increased to 490,000. By the time Eddie took his oath to the USMC the war had escalated with dreadful consequences as 11,364 soldiers had been killed in action in 1967.

In another twist of fate, Chris was heading to Vietnam, too.

Two weeks later, on a summer day with her heart heavy, but also filled with great pride, Jane waved farewell to her only son. Eddie, handsome, tall, and blond, and so very young, sat in the car that his pretty girlfriend Rona was driving. Rona's long, dark, silky tresses were blowing from the car window, as strains of the Beatles "*Hey Jude*" blared forth from the radio. The young couple enthusiastically waved goodbye to Jane together. They were headed to Camp

Lejeune, the Marine Corps boot camp and training base in North Carolina. Jane stood waving back until Rona's faded blue Thunderbird disappeared in the distance.

She thought about how fast the past seven years had flown by. Max was gone now six years, Mama who had been by Jane's side during her most difficult time decided to return to Germany a year earlier to spend her senior years back in the old country with Karl, and Eddie was heading to Southeast Asia. It seemed like just a few weeks had passed when Eddie, then age ten, walked into the kitchen one day and announced in loud voice, "Mom, I got engaged today!"

"What!" replied his mother, feigning mock surprise, "Is it that serious?"

"Oh no," Eddie casually replied, "we're just going steadily" a term the kids were using at the time for dating.

But as time went on, Eddie and Rona would remain together, eventually announcing real plans for getting married, once he returned home from Vietnam.

Jane realized that she was on her own. Both men in her life were overseas serving their country, the country that she had come to love so much.

With all that in mind, Jane turned to God for guidance as she had so many times before, asking for patience and the safe return of her son. She prayed as only a mother can for their child. She also prayed for Chris, who had become so important to her, prayed for her own mother, who had been so helpful and strong for Jane throughout her life.

CHAPTER SIXTEEN

Reunion

With a great mixture of anticipation, anxiety, and dread, Jane watched the big DC-3 land and start to taxi down the runway of the small Newcastle Airport.

So much had changed in the past year, much of it for the better. It was now 1968, and while the Vietnam War was still raging, both Eddie and Chris were out of harm's way, which brought Jane a great measure of relief.

Eddie had returned home safely, but not before he and the Marine battalion he was attached to conquered "Hill 55" in a fierce battle and hard-fought victory. Eddie claimed the mound for Delaware by firmly planting a state flag that Rona had sent him from home on top of the hill. Someone took a picture of that glorious moment and Jane swelled with a great sense of pride when she saw it published in the local newspapers. Incredibly, one-time Chris actually communicated with Eddie from his scout plane when he flew over Eddie's position (a conversation Eddie took quite a ribbing for as he was a Private First Class and Chris was wearing officer insignia as Major.)

Shortly after he made his way back home Eddie and Rona were married, fulfilling a promise he made so many years before as a boy.

Chris had made it through the war unscathed, and Jane would be seeing him get off that big silver plane in just a few moments. He had already made a short visit to his folks and siblings in Washington State and now a homecoming of sorts for the two of them.

Jane was so nervous as she stood waiting. She was so worried to tell Chris about the multiple sclerosis that her great anticipation of his arrival was mixed with a sense of dread about his response.

Jane looked stunning standing there in the bright sunshine in her body hugging sea blue and white striped dress, high heels, and hair floating in easy curls down to her shoulders. She had done an incredible job of holding her emotions in check and controlling her heart that was bursting with expectation and excitement. Yet the agony of having to tell him about her diagnosis of MS was almost too much to bear.

But then, she saw him.

Tall, blond, and with that defined military walk, almost a march of sorts that comes as a byproduct of being a career United States Air Force officer, Chris made his way to Jane and they hugged.

It was a long, emotional hug. She gripped Chris by his broad shoulders and dug her face into his chest. They stood there silently embracing each other for a very long time, unaware they were standing in an airport.

The fact that he had returned home to her gave Jane a sudden renewed sense of inner strength and courage and in almost pragmatic tones she whispered, "Chris, I have bad news to tell you. I have multiple sclerosis. I was diagnosed in 1967, but…well…I just couldn't summon the strength to tell you."

She pushed back from him a bit and looked at him questioningly, waiting for his response.

Chris said nothing. His steel blue eyes registered no reaction to Jane's big news. Then, in that moment of silence, Jane started to question her own feelings about her illness. Was she overdoing it with fears and concerns? What about Chris who had just escaped from real battles and dangers in the war in Vietnam as he flew his O2 "Bird Dog" scout plane over enemy positions, risking his own life many times a day? What about the emotional toll on Chris from flying the amazing little two seat Cessna sized plane with its front and rear props that allowed for stunning maneuvers to avoid getting hit from the enemy flack launched at him from the ground? He put his life on the line over and over again, being shot at so he could release a small targeted smoke bomb and then call in the heavy hitters - the bombers – and commanding them to "hit my smoke!" The bomber squadron would then pinpoint the target and do their job.

As a result of one of those missions, Chris was awarded the Silver Star, the United States military's third highest personal decoration for valor in combat and here she was worrying about MS.

As they took a few minutes over a cup of coffee to continue catching up Jane asked if Chris could stay. The coffee lounge suddenly seemed a very sobering place as he answered her question, "No, Jane, I cannot stay. Matter of fact my plane leaves in twenty minutes. I have to be at a scheduled meeting in London tomorrow."

Jane set down her coffee cup with a heavy sigh. Chris took her hand in his and said, "I will write at my earliest possible chance. I promise."

After a brief embrace and a promising look from Chris he walked away towards the military plane that was waiting and he soon disappeared through the doors that closed behind him.

Jane kept waving goodbye until his plane faded from sight over the distant horizon.

****

A new ray of hope and encouragement engulfed Jane when her first letter arrived from Chris. He sounded so upbeat about his assignment in Germany as he explained how his schedule with the Douglas C-133 aircraft was keeping him flying almost non-stop. The rest of the letter was very benign and non-committal. True to his word, Chris always wrote regularly, but never a word about any future plans for them.

Although there had been no conversation between them about Jane's health problems she intuitively felt, on some level, that her life with Chris was not over as she had secretly feared. She wouldn't blame him one bit, however, if he decided to close the door between them forever. What kind of life would it be for an Air Force officer with an invalid wife?

As the letters from Chris were always welcomed, Jane was beginning to lose hope that they would ever have a future together and the words of Dr. Musser *"Bing...Bing...Bing..."* were never far away from her.

One day she finally decided that before she ended up in a wheelchair she was going to see more of the world, so she booked a trip to Morocco.

The very next morning Jane was seated at her desk when her telephone rang.

"Jane," Beulah, the telephone operator said excitedly, "I hear you're going to Morocco! I would do anything to go, would you take me with you?"

"Wow!" said Jane, "News sure travels fast around here, how did you hear about it already?"

"Your line was busy when your travel agent called so she asked me to let you know that your tickets are ready and would be sending them over by messenger early this afternoon."

After a short pause, Beulah asked again. "Well, what about it? Would you let me go with you?"

"Of course," Jane agreed, "under one condition…" and before she could explain her friend interrupted.

"Anything," replied Beulah, "I will carry your suitcase, since I know you have this MS thing and cannot carry anything heavy. Besides, you'll be doing all the driving because I don't know how to drive!"

Jane said, "You took the words right out of my mouth! You haul the luggage and I'll do the driving!"

Together and as if on cue, Jane and Beulah laughed out loud and before the day was over, Jane was proudly waving two tickets for a trip to Morocco.

CHATPER SEVENTEEN
Morocco

Time passed quickly and before they knew it Jane and Beulah were off on their adventure. But before the girls made it to Morocco they decided to begin their trip on the southeast coast of France on the Mediterranean Sea, at the foot of the Alps.

Equipped with a copy of the latest AAA travel book, "Europe On Five Dollars a Day," Jane and Beulah set out from Nice, France, in their little rented Renault. They bounced down the road along the French Riviera towards Monte Carlo enjoying the breathtaking views and the opportunities to stop and take pictures of people, places…and a camel.

"Look!" said Beulah excitedly, "What in the world is that camel doing right here in the middle of this beautiful city of Monaco where Princess Grace and Prince Rainier live?"

"I'm wondering about that camel myself," said Jane who had a puzzled look on her face. "It looks like an Arab Bedouin leading that camel. Let's take a closer look."

The Bedouin didn't speak English, but for the price of one shiny new Kennedy silver coin he invited the girls to climb aboard his grunting, kneeling animal.

What a grand adventure it was as the two friends had great fun aboard the beast, including a ride along a portion of the famed "Grand Prix" racing strip, something they were both sure no one back at the office had ever experienced before! They finally dismounted from the camel near the front door of the famous Monte Carlo Casino.

Beulah could hardly contain her excitement but stopped short at the entrance of the impressive looking casino doors when she glanced back and saw the cautionary look on Jane's face.

"Well, it's just to tell everyone back home that we have been inside, Jane. I mean the camel was great but this…will make an even better story, for sure!" said Beulah with an encouraging smile.

Jane was quickly convinced and with a slight nod of agreement they entered the massive palatial structure that was world renowned since its doors opened in 1863, attracting the rich and famous with its high stakes gambling, ornate interior, and lush gardens.

The shouts of "Banco!" from the croupier drew them closer to the crowd milling around a large gambling table, signaling that betting was closed as he began raking in the high stakes. Mesmerized by all that was going on and forgetting that they had just spent time on a camel, both Jane and Beulah suddenly realized that they were way out of their league, and one look around confirmed it. The ladies in attendance were resplendent in high fashion gowns and men in tuxedos made them acutely aware of how shabby and "touristy" they must look…not to mention the smell of that camel.

With smiles on their faces they quickly left, making their way back to the little Renault. They made good time driving through the peaceful countryside of France and even had time for a lunch stop in Marseilles to taste their famous Bouillabaisse or "fish soup."

It had been quite a morning.

They made their way to Barcelona and found it a very large and exciting experience. Consulting their trusty, dusty AAA booklet once more they decided to visit the Casa Milá designed by the famed architect and sculptor Antoni Gaudí.

"Way out!" was the favorite expression Jane and Beulah used to describe the relic of surrealistic artistry throughout the building. It was simply incredible. They absolutely had to explore the place.

At dinner that night, Jane and Beulah were fortunate enough to meet a descendant of Gaudí's, a Señora de Meridia. She was an elegant woman who looked every bit like a classic Spanish Contessa. This meeting was one of the many ways this adventure became the trip of a lifetime.

From Barcelona to Valencia, through all the cities and towns along the way to the seaport of Algeciras at the very tip of Spain where they drove in the little Renault, Jane and Beulah were stared at constantly because they were the only women drivers. They were a curious sight for the locals, especially for the women who walked alongside their pack mules and also to the men riding on mules.

At one point in the trip the "animal traffic" became very heavy as men were prodding herds of goats along their route and in one instance it was a vast flock of sheep being moved uphill which blocked Jane's driving lane. When she saw the chance (after much care and calculation) to pass them she maneuvered the little car around the animals, however, out of sight just beyond the crest of the hill sat a motorcycle cop who promptly pulled them over.

There was a serious lapse in communication from English to Spanish between them, except for the words the officer kept repeating.

"Seven thousand pesetas…seven thousand pesetas!"

"That sounds like an awful lot of money that we don't have," said Jane. When they refused to pay the fine, the motorcycle cop motioned them to follow and led the way to the local Police Department. The desk Sargent at the station was neither understanding nor accommodating to the foreigners. In rough tones he barked out a litany of Spanish words neither Jane or Beulah could understand, and every sentence seemed to end with, "Seven thousand pesetas."

In short order, the two women were put behind bars. They had become outlaws for passing a flock of sheep!

Dumbfounded and at a loss they began to assess their situation. "Look at us! How could two American women suddenly wind up in a Spanish jail? How long do you think they can keep us here?" Beulah uttered with more than a little bit of concern in her voice.

Jane, perplexed as well, said, "I don't know, but I'm getting very hungry, its already past supper time. Don't they have to feed their prisoners? Maybe I'll just ask the guard."

"Don't be so callous, Jane, we're in enough trouble as it is. We should have just waited for those sheep to move out of the way."

"Just a little gallows humor," chuckled Jane.

While they were discussing their fate and the hunger pangs in their bellies, they heard the familiar clanking of keys unlock the heavy iron door down the hall. The girls looked quizzically at each other at what they saw next.

Marching down the hallway towards them was a short, stocky older man in a blue Spanish uniform of sorts, with many citations, sashes, and endless medals crisscrossing his chest.

"Town mayor?" asked Beulah.

"Nope," said Jane with a smirk, "They are sending us Pancho Villa!"

With that, the stocky man spun on his heels and

stomped away!

A few minutes later, the motorcycle cop appeared once again and announced in a half Spanish, half English tone "You are free to leave."

The girls didn't waste a moment getting out of the cell and bolted to freedom. The cop even held the door of the Renault open for them, which prompted Jane to throw him a kiss, just like Dinah Shore always did at the end of her television show.

"That's enough of that, Jane." Beulah exclaimed, taking hold of her friend's hand and pulling her into the car. "Let's get outta here before they lock us up and throw away the keys!"

****

The next few days had the girls heading towards the exotic city of Tangier in Morocco, eager to explore its rich and fascinating history as the gateway between Africa and Europe in ancient times. They took a ferry boat that brought them across the Straits of Gibraltar to the African continent, whereupon they were greeted by a gentleman wearing a long grey robe and a red fez as they disembarked from the boat.

He was tall and thin with a wisp of beard, a mysterious and imposing figure if there ever was one.

"My name is Mohammad Farouk," he announced with an air of great confidence. "I am here to help you change your money and be your guide as long as you are guests of the Hotel Rif."

Jane and Beulah let out an audible sigh of relief. For a moment they expected the man to be a shady character, a spy perhaps or undercover agent straight from the script of the movie "Casablanca."

"How considerate of the hotel," said Jane. "But tell me Monsieur Farouk, how did you pick us out so easily from this great crowd of people?" she inquired, still hoping for a bit of intrigue at their meeting.

Flashing a broad smile with gleaming white teeth that were in sharp contrast to his dark eyes, Farouk laughed out loud. "Two American women getting off the boat? Not very difficult Miss."

They all had a good chuckle as they boarded the dusty taxi towards the hotel. Monsieur Farouk would be their guide for the length of their stay as a courtesy from the hotel.

The next five days in Tangier were exceptional, riveting and mysterious. The exotic smells of the very best spices in the open market was intoxicating to Jane and Beulah. The smokers huddled in secluded corners smoking opium pipes were a sight to behold. The dazzling array of meats for sale and vendors who filled the streets with a stunning array of copper and silver trinkets along with vast piles of handmade clothing was almost too much of a temptation not to fill their bags for the trip home.

The place was vital and alive, and it filled Jane with a deep sense of wonder and appreciation for the journey she had taken, staying true to herself and following her instincts about "seeing the world" before she might not be able to.

On the very last day of their adventure, they traveled to an outlying area where gypsies dwelled in caves peddling their freshly sheared lamb's wool that was on display in large, open baskets perched on rocks and boulders. As promised, Monsieur Farouk was always nearby giving the girls a sense of safety which allowed them to explore without fear and he even led them past the gypsies to a large dark cave, about the length of a football field, that he called "The Caves of Hercules." Entering the sacred stone cathedral, the girls could clearly see the outline of a man's head at the far end of the cave and the breathtaking view of the vast blue and green Mediterranean Sea.

Farouk explained that in Greek mythology Hercules used his superhuman strength to smash through the rock and, by doing so, he connected the Atlantic Ocean to the Mediterranean Sea forming the Strait of Gibraltar.

In that moment, Jane thought of how far apart she was from Chris and wondered again if they would ever be together.

She would soon have her answer.

CHAPTER EIGHTEEN

Beginnings

Jane had just decided against spending the day at the beach with her ski club friends and before she could call them the phone rang. It was Chris.

"Chris, where are you? Should I come to the airport to pick you up? I was going to go to the beach, but I changed my mind and glad I did otherwise I might have missed your call and…"

"Hold everything Jane," Chris interjected. "I'm still in Europe but have plans to be back in the United States by this coming Friday. So, don't make any plans because we are getting married. We can get the marriage license when I arrive. Clean out your apartment on Saturday, we'll get married on Sunday, and then we'll both return to Ramstein AFB on Monday. So, get busy and liquidate everything you really don't need because we can't bring anything with us. We have everything we need right here at the base."

The conversation went on for thirty minutes, most of it was hazy as Jane could hardly comprehend what was actually happening. They said goodbye and hung up the phone.

Jane stood for a moment, in total silence not really sure what had just taken place. "I think he just proposed to me," she murmured with a slight smile on her face.

Without any regard to protocol or her surroundings or condition, Jane ran down the steps from her apartment that led out to a small garden area and with arms stretched to the heavens, she loudly screamed out, "YIPPEE!"

One deep breath, followed by a few clumsy dance steps expressed her joy, her deep love for Chris, and how blessed she felt in that moment. She swayed slowly in the sunlight, basking in the glory of God, her prayers being answered, and her path taking another turn.

September 6, 1970 was a glorious fall day the perfect backdrop for *Jane Horten* to become *Mrs. Jane Johnson*, but just before the ceremony on that special Sunday in Wilmington Jane pulled Chris aside and asked him a very important question.

"Chris, I am so very happy that we are getting married, but I have to know something. Ever since I was diagnosed with MS my fear has been that you wouldn't accept me as a whole woman, that I would be less than, damaged goods somehow. But even when I confided in you my deepest fear, you said nothing about it. Why did you accept me as you did?

Her words hung in the air for a few moments between them. The question was a long time in coming and Chris knew that an answer was important and needed in that moment.

"Soon enough you will meet my sister Anne. She is near and dear to me and was also diagnosed with MS years before you Jane. I learned that her 'disability' is in name only and while she has had many challenges, she continues to overcome them with great strength. I see that same strength in you and so to answer your question, you are a whole person to me, the one person I want to spend the rest of my life with."

Jane was overcome with emotion. Once again, God had put things in order, even before she knew of them, there was a Divine Plan for her life as there had always been, and this was another piece of that Plan.

The ceremony was just as it should be with her son Eddie as the best man and his wife Rona was the best woman and when Jane heard Chris say, *"for better or for worse"* she knew it wasn't just a few words repeated by rote. It was a declaration of unconditional love from her husband and the coming years would prove her right.

There was a small informal luncheon served after the ceremony, but there was little time to celebrate. The next day "The Johnsons" would be leaving for Germany. Chris still had a year left at Ramstein AFB before he would move on to his next and last assignment at Eglin AFB in Florida.

Life moved forward quickly as Chris's military tour continued but being back in Germany was bittersweet to Jane on so many levels. Germany would always be her homeland, but so much had changed since she grew up in Munich, much of it for the better. Often the splinters of the past would work their way to the surface and rather than pull them out, many times Jane just buried the pain and pushed them back in.

But there were many bright spots as well. Chris' military tour was both busy and exciting and Jane was able to take university courses offered on the base. A memorable time happened when Chris seized the opportunity for a special assignment to Norway and was able to take Jane with him. During a break from his duties, for the first time, he was able to meet some of his "Viking ancestor" relatives who were living around the Geiranger Fjord.

The morning after arriving, Chris, his cousin Arne, and several hearty kin folk set out on a steep hike into the surrounding mountains. The climb was tough yet exhilarating and refreshing. They stopped just long enough to enjoy the cold clear water that streamed from underground through make-shift drinking fountains made of stone.

When they reached the summit, Arne pointed out a small cabin like structure that he called the "Huitter." He explained in half Norwegian and half English that this was a resting spot for climbers to spend the night and eat breakfast before heading back down the mountain. They enjoyed the provisions that were left to them by previous hikers and, in the ongoing spirit of the place, contributed generously to the collection bucket held by Elias the "Huitter-Keeper" to replace provisions for those who would follow.

Later, when Chris and Jane drove back up to see the Geiranger Fjord together, they happened to see a rainbow that arched across the fjord from one end to the other, so close that Jane could touch the end of the rainbow. Jane joked about looking for the proverbial "pot of gold," but she already knew in her heart that her life was being filled up with great treasures of the Spirit. It was overflowing with blessings from God and in this time of new beginnings there were more great adventures to come.

CHAPTER NINETEEN

Space A

"Jane, we have a guest for dinner!" Chris announced as he walked through the door of their apartment located in Otterbach, a little hamlet not far from the gates of Ramstein AFB.

"Jane, come and meet Leo!"

Jane wiped her hands on her apron and quickly made her way to the living room and there was Chris with very tall, handsome man standing next to him wearing a flight jacket and big smile on his face.

"Jane, meet Leo...Leo meet Jane," Chris said. "Leo and I met in 'Nam and he is one of the best of the best. I was bragging on your great German cooking and guess what? Leo is from Austria!"

Jane could tell that the two men shared a great respect for each other and, in mere moments, also found out that both she and Leo spoke the same dialect!

It was an incredible dinner with great conversation in two languages. After the meal was consumed Leo sat back in his chair and thanked Jane for the amazing "board of fare" then made an announcement.

"I have been assigned to pilot a "Space A"[10] flight to Athens next week. How would you two like to tag along for the ride? I can arrange it if you are interested."

It took Jane less than ten seconds to respond.

"I'm always ready for an adventure, Leo," she said. "I absolutely love exploring the world, new sights, and sounds, just ask Chris," who nodded in agreement. Then Jane smiled broadly and said, "Especially at the price of a Space Available flight. So, count me in!"

One-week later Chris and Jane watched from the hanger entrance as Leo and other flight suit clad pilots went through their last-minute inspections on the massive C-47 that sat on the apron, engines idling. After some quick introductions Mark, the loadmaster, waved a hasty hello then disappeared into an opening in the underbelly of the fuselage. Leo gave a quick snap salute to indicate "we're ready for take-off, get on board!"

Jane limped towards the steps to climb onboard the

---

[10] Space A (Space Available) flight is offered to United States Uniformed Services members when a flight is not fully booked with passengers traveling under orders.

aircraft - her full leg brace was no hindrance to climbing up the steps one leg at a time. (She always wore the brace as a precaution during excursions and long walks.)

After the passengers were seated Jane suddenly remembered another time years before when she flew in a C-47 airship as a war bride. That C-47's seating configuration was designed to accommodate the many War Brides, but this flight had bench seats running the length of the fuselage, some spaces occupied by U.S. servicemen, still others by more "Space A" travelers.

The big plane with its human and other cargo rumbled down the runway picking up speed and soon enough was pushing its nose into the wind, climbing altitude quickly. The plane had been in the air about 20 minutes or so with passengers huddling together in an attempt to keep warm (the C-47 is not known for their heating capacity) when Jane spied a familiar head of flaming red hair. It belonged to a friend named Diana who was with her husband Norman, a fellow member of Chris's squadron. Instinctively Diana looked back and caught Jane's gaze and gave her a friendly smile.

Mark, the loadmaster, suddenly appeared near the cockpit. He approached Jane directly and shouted to her over the roar of the engines, "Would you like to see a mid-air re-fueling?"

Jane strained to hear his words, but quickly gave him a "thumbs-up," and yelled, "YES!" Mark then pointed to a ladder leading up to the cockpit.

With Mark keeping a wary eye on Jane, she cautiously maneuvered up the ladder in her full leg brace. Half way up she stopped suddenly and stood still in awe of what she was seeing before her. Over a row of computers manned by pilots who were simultaneously observing through the windows above them, Jane could see another plane flying just a few feet above the one she was on, matching its speed perfectly!

Then a large hose appeared into view, snaking its way down from the higher plane reaching toward a hose that was rising up from the plane Jane was on, and in a miracle of avi-ation and technology, the two hoses finally connected and the refueling began, giving the C-47 more fuel to complete its flight. After a few minutes Jane turned and looked down the ladder she was standing on and saw Mark motioning her to descend the steps.

In a high velocity voice, he bellowed, "Better come down now. Pilots aren't used to an audience, and we don't want them getting nervous."

Jane took her seat, looked at Chris and smiled, then snuggled in as close as she could to keep warm for the duration of the flight.

It was about six o'clock in Athens by the time the "Space A" group found their way into the treasure laden ancient city in Greece. The weather was ideal for exploring and the fellow travelers soon found themselves in a small city park which was situated just below the famed Acropolis.

Exhausted from their wanderings, they spied a vacant bench nearby and with a deep sense of relief plopped down for a breather.

It was Diana who spoke first, "I don't know about all of you but I'm starving," she exclaimed, tossing her formidable red mane of hair in punctuation of her remark. They all quickly agreed with the need for food and without a word among them, silently headed for a Restaurant/Hotel sign just across the street from the park.

The place is quaint and comfortable like a mom & pop type of restaurant we have back home in the United States, Jane thought. But when they were seated and attempted to read their choices they hit a snag as they hesitated and mumbled their way through the strange language on the menus. "It's literally all Greek to me," grumbled Tom who was seated at the head of the table. Searching the faces of his companions he asked, "So…who is going to order for us?"

After a slight hesitation, Brenda suddenly shouted out, "Hey, let Jane order, she speaks German! I think we should let her do the ordering!"

A bit startled, Jane responded with, "You've got to be kidding me!" Her companions however were having none of it and slowly shook their heads with mock sad faces and sorrowful eyes. Even Chris joined in the group guilt trip and slowly shook his head, even though he sported a smirk that turned into a grin.

Defiantly Jane announced, "Okay, you asked for it!" and rose from her seat and headed off to the kitchen, smiled at the cook and introduced herself. One look at the friendly little woman wearing a starched apron and broad smile with twinkling eyes and Jane was instantly reminded of kind old Kuni, who had given her and Gretchen those two cold boiled potatoes so many years before at Castle Waldkrone.

Jane quickly took charge of the situation. Looking around she noticed a great number of cast iron pots on the massive cast iron stove used for cooking great quantities at one time. She reached out and lifted the lid of one of the many pots and the aroma of red beets and potatoes floated up and filled the kitchen. Jane took a plate from a nearby shelf and motioned the cook to deposit the wonderful concoction on the plate and then continued on to other pots on the stove, making her choices and filling the plate in the process. Although there was no conversation between them, the little cook and Jane had silent communication and six more plates were filled to perfection with identical cuisine.

Jane then returned to her friends, acting as server, doling out the steaming plates of food and while smacking her lips in delight uttered, "Go ahead and taste the total piquancy of these fine morsels, because that's what you're getting for dinner…like it or not!"

No greater dinner could be had that night than the one shared by these friends as the food was savored with delight, the conversation was upbeat and carefree between the "Space A'ers." Just before they all headed to their hotel rooms for the night the fiery Diana announced to all that she would like to be called by her new Greek name "Artemis" until further notice.

Everyone had a belly laugh and bade each other good-night.

The next morning was a flurry of activity after finally at the airport Mark and Leo announced that the plane was loaded and ready for take-off. The next assignment was Turkey. Mark offered up the chance to continue on with, "If anybody would like to go, here is your chance to see Istanbul. We're leaving shortly."

The group was ready for another adventure, but Chris cut through the excitement, "Thanks for the invite but I am running out of time and need to get back to Frankfurt." He continued, "Actually, we've lucked out. The next 'Space A' flight is leaving for Frankfurt at noon, Jane and I have to be on it."

"Good luck and safe flight!" Leo shouted to his friend, as he ascended into the C-47 to claim his pilot seat. "I'll see you back at Ramstein!"

With that, Chris and Jane made their way back to Germany where he would spend one more year and then go on serve out his time in the Air Force at his final duty station at Eglin AFB in Florida. Chris retired in 1972 as a Major after serving with distinction for 20 years.

CHAPTER TWENTY

Teacher

After Chris retired from the Air Force, the very next day he reported for duty at a Real Estate Brokerage firm. He traded in his flight suit for a business suit and applied the same discipline, focus, and military bearing he had in the military to business life. While he missed being in the air, he did like a challenge and quickly adapted and succeeded in his new chosen field of endeavor.

Jane and Chris soon settled into the small community of Choctaw Woods, overlooking the beautiful Thomson Bayou. They soon became accustomed to the glorious Florida sunsets, as most evenings the sky was painted with a kaleidoscope of red, pink, and purple showing off their glory as mirrored in the waters of the bayou.

Life was good.

With help from the wife of another retired USAF officer Jane was able to become part of a small volunteer group that was teaching English to foreign-born students at a local Baptist Church.

For three years the Johnsons made their way in the

world, the military years fading behind them. But the Fall of Saigon on April 30, 1975 not only signaled the end of the Vietnam War, but also would put Jane right back in the thick of things at Eglin AFB. She would join a cadre of volunteers and teachers that were charged with teaching English to a vast sea of Vietnamese refugees in "tent city" (which was a swath of 500 tents set up in less than a week by 1,200 people who were pulled from their regular duty). It was set up to house, teach, and shelter up to 10,000 refugees until it was forced to be closed by Hurricane Eloise in September of 1975.

Jane found the work rewarding, giving, and her natural ability to teach was instrumental in helping those whose country had been torn apart by war. Jane knew first-hand what it took to understand and become part of a new culture, which she experienced many years earlier.

Her teaching continued in 1977 when she was offered a position to teach German in a local, private Christian academy. At first it was a struggle for Jane because she had to write her own curriculum but then, miraculously, the Bob Jones Christian Academy stepped in and offered to let them buy needed classroom materials and after that it was smooth sailing. Her students became immersed in the language and soon enough, after much prayer and planning, Jane and four of her students were able to actually go to Germany.

Once again Jane was returning to the land she loved so very much. Just before they left, Matthew, the only male student on the trip shook hands with Chris and assured him that he would watch out for Jane's well-being. As in the past, Jane often relied on a wheel chair for long field trips and this one would be no different.

On their itinerary was a trip up the Rhine River. They disembarked in St. Goar and while making their way up to Castle Kanz, Jane could hear her charges behind her whispering and making "*shhh*" sounds. Something was clearly going on.

"Girls! Matthew! Come up in front of me where I can see you. What is going on back there? What are you not telling me?" snapped Jane.

The girls jumped at Jane's orders immediately, but another stronger nudge was needed, "Matthew, that means you too!"

As soon as Matthew let go of Jane's wheelchair, she began to instantly feel herself leaning to one side, as one of the tires in her wheelchair had sprung a leak!

"Oh Matthew, Anna, Wendy, Susan, I am so sorry. I thought you were up to no good. I had no idea I was running out of air!" Not too worried about the leaking tire, Jane spied a small building not far away, so she continued, "I've got an idea. See that post office right down there? I am going to show you how to make a long-distance call, so we can call the school and talk with everyone right from here!" Checking her watch Jane confirmed that school would still be in session back in Florida.

"Yay!" Shouted the students in unison, and they began counting their expense money in Deutsche Marks. In just a few moments they were all making their way down the hill, the girls carefully supporting Jane as she walked and Matthew pushed the wheel chair with its flat tire towards the town.

They explored the post office and made the call to school and then took turns saying hello. Matthew went first, but then suddenly vanished. After a delightful conversation,

Jane and the girls left the small building and suddenly spotted Matthew who was whistling down a kid on a bike who had a tire repair kit strapped under his bicycle seat! Jane and the girls drew closer just in time to hear Matthew speak to the boy and ask for his help in fixing the flat!

"Mein Freund, können wir borgen Ihr Fahrrad Reifen Reparatur Kit umser Lehrerin zu helfen?" (My Friend, can we use your bicycle tire repair kit to help our teacher?) Matthew's German was not quite perfect, but it got the job done and Jane was so very proud of her student.

The young boy quickly agreed once he saw Jane's predicament and in no time at all she was "rolling again."

This was cause for celebration! Matthew had gotten an "A" in the field test!

The little group made its way to a nearby "Gaststätte" (restaurant) which gave them all another chance to put their new language skills to use. Jane beamed at her students and they all enjoyed a hearty laugh about how the day had unfolded and the ingenuity of Matthew (who smiled for the rest of the trip). He made good on his promise to Chris to look out for his teacher's welfare, which was in some ways a preview that was showcasing his talents as a future lawyer.

The next three weeks passed quickly, during which time Jane had many thoughts about the "full circle moments" that brought her back to her homeland Germany. She fondly recalled her return with Chris at Ramstein and now with these young people as their teacher, something she could have never imagined when she left for America in 1948.

When they finally returned home the stories about their adventures were passed around to family and friends for a very long time. For Jane, that time with her students, back home in Germany, was a revival of that deep sense of "*Gemuetlichkeit*" that had eroded over the years but was now becoming stronger in her spirit.

CHAPTER TWENTY-ONE

Free Fall

It was 1999. Twenty-two years had passed since the trip to Germany, much of it filled with family and friends and one of Jane's favorite things was to visit Eddie and Rona in Delaware. It was there that she would finally be invited to fulfill a long-held dream.

Unbeknownst to Jane just as she was pulling into Eddie and Rona's driveway their telephone rang. When Eddie answered his face lit up, "Leo! What a pleasant surprise! My mom? No, she just stepped out for a few…but wait I think I hear her car in the driveway…hold on a minute."

Jane walked in the door of her son's house with a big smile on her face that only got wider once she picked up the phone. "Well hello, Leo, what's up? How did you know where to reach me?"

Leo was more than enthusiastic on the other end of the line. "Chris told me you were spending time with Eddie and Rona in Delaware. But I didn't call just to say 'Hi!' Jane, you have got to drop whatever you are doing and come to Kansas City. The weather here has never been more ideal for parachuting and guys are chuting left and right. The thought came to me that it was time to keep my promise to you, to let you know when conditions were perfect for you to 'free fall'…remember?"

"Of course, I remember, Leo," said Jane. "I've been waiting for this call for a long time, my friend."

"Well, now is your chance, Jane. But don't delay your departure, in two more days I have to be back to the business of flying. This time I'm taking the 747 to deliver a large cargo of pregnant cows to Turkey."

Jane laughed out loud at the thought of a plane full of bovines mooing their way to Turkey with Leo at the controls.

"I am on my way, Leo. See you soon!"

After making a few arrangements Jane was flying out of the Philadelphia airport winging her way towards Kansas City. Sitting in the plane at 35,000 feet, she couldn't help but admire the view but the thought of jumping out of a plane at 10,000 feet and "flying" back to the earth was giving her a mix of emotions, with excitement beyond description at the top of the list.

At the age of seventy plus, it would be her first time to do a parachute jump.

Looking back out of the window, so many thoughts were crowding her mind it was hard to sit still, but eventually the constant droning of the jet engines acted like a brain balm and she fell asleep.

Just three hours later Jane was sitting in a Jeep with Leo at the wheel heading towards Independence, Missouri and "The Flyers Club." When they arrived, the small private airfield was filled with activity, the perfect weather conditions bringing out throngs of skydivers. Men, women, old, and young all paced about in their jumpsuits waiting for the next available aircraft that would send them aloft, only to leap into the wind and plummet towards earth. This was a thrill that Jane was ready to experience!

Jane counted three Cessna 182 Skylane aircraft with their engines roaring waiting in line for take-off with another group of air explorers, but soon her attention was drawn to a large makeshift hangar that she found herself gravitating towards.

When her eyes adjusted from the brilliant sunshine outside to the slightly darker interior of the large hanger, there was a group of people dressed in jumpsuits, with parachutes strapped to their backs ready for their next adventure. A few others were busily repacking spent parachutes for future jumps and in passing she noted guys sporting flip-flops, not shoes or sneakers. To one side there was a rack of jump suits hanging, so Jane grabbed one that would accommodate her petite five-foot two-inch size frame. She slipped it on and it fit like it had been custom made for her!

Then Leo and another man, already clad in their jumping gear, entered the hanger. Leo got right to the introductions, "Jane, meet your tandem instructor Ino Rasmussen, the best instructor anywhere around."

Jane was hyped and raring to go, "Nice to meet you, Ino. Can we go now? I'm ready!" she exclaimed.

Ino (who was used to the ramped-up emotions of first time jumpers) interjected quickly, "Not so fast, Jane. First we need to talk and sign a few papers before we get on that plane."

The trio headed for the small make-shift office in the corner of the tent. Leo stationed himself in the extra chair, ready for any friendly support if needed, and after the usual list of questions about weight, height and age Ino looked Jane directly in the eyes.

"I saw you limping while you walked. Why is that?" he asked.

The question was certainly unexpected and went right to Jane's biggest fears about "being less than" when it came to important matters.

"Oh no!" she thought to herself, "He's never going to let me jump if I tell him." She gave Ino a puzzled look and glanced back at Leo, while she shrugged her shoulders.

"Well...tell him," said Leo with a reassuring grin.

Jane squared her shoulders, sat up as tall as possible and strongly declared, "I have multiple sclerosis!"

"Oh, is that all?" Ino blurted out sounding almost relieved. "We have a paraplegic that jumps with us all the time and we actually have to help propel him out of his wheelchair as he makes the jump and then we bring him his chair once he lands."

With a pained smile *and* a grateful heart, Jane said, "Well then, there is hope for me after all!"

After a few more instructions Ino added, "At about 10,000 feet we will propel out of the plane and be on our way to free fall. Then when 'it's time' I will tap you on the head three times, then you'll feel a small jerking sensation and that's when the chute will open."

Ino paused a moment to let his instructions linger in the air and then added, "If you come down dead, it's nobody's fault. Not yours, not ours, nobody's. Do you understand, Jane?"

After another moment of silence to let his words sink in, Ino asked the question that Jane had been waiting to hear for years.

"Ready to jump?" he queried.

"Yes, I am," Jane responded barely able to contain herself.

Ino eyed his student closely and said, "So if you have no questions and are good to go then sign this form."

Jane picked up the pen, thought for a moment and said, "Well, there is one more thing, one *very important thing.*"

"Sure," said Ino. "What is it?"

"I would like to say a prayer to God to send his Holy Angels along to guide and protect us this morning."

Right then and there they huddled up, prayed, and just a few minutes later it was "*one...two...three!*"

Jane was launched out of the safety of the Cessna into the greatest thrill of her life and with her arms outstretched like an eagle, she was flying through the air with Ino as her guide, while another jumper sporting a camera filmed their free fall from high above the earth.

It was a feeling of freedom she had never experienced before.

Soon enough, she felt Ino give her the expected three taps on the head and suddenly they began "potato chipping" through the air, with nothing to hold them up. It was just a streamer (a chute that fails to open,) but then all at once there was a heavy tug from above as predicated and, in an instant, everything became still in a cloudless, totally silent descent through the atmosphere.

Jane was simply floating as if suspended in time and space, but her peaceful thoughts were suddenly interrupted by Ino who had a measured dose of urgency in his voice.

"We just had a malfunction. The chute did not open, and we are now on the emergency chute and two miles off of our drop zone," he announced.

Jane looked down and could clearly see the highway below where cars and trucks were speeding along on the concrete. The small back-up chute was dropping them much too fast and even though this was potentially a very serious situation she was inexplicably devoid of any fear or anxiety and a sense of calm washed over her.

"PULL UP YOUR LEGS!" shouted Ino, "PULL UP! PULL UP!"

Jane concentrated on doing exactly what her instructor was demanding, but her legs had been a weak point for so long and now he was insisting that she somehow find the strength to move them as never before. She pushed every ounce of energy into her lower body while at the same time reaching her arms upward crying, "Where are the steering ropes?"

"No steering ropes on a back-up chute," snapped Ino. "We are at the mercy of the winds."

The ground kept getting bigger and bigger below them as they swayed back and forth, the smaller chute straining a bit under the pull of gravity and the weight of the two sky-divers.

It was a rough landing to say the least but, thankfully, they had been blown away from the highway and into a muddy field where they splashed down, the wet ground cushioning their fall.

"You alright, Jane?"

"Yes, I'm okay, Ino. Are you okay?"

After a quick check for broken bones and possible concussion they both took a deep sigh of relief. No injuries but each took a moment to catch their breath.

*What a ride…*but not one Jane wanted to repeat any time soon.

Ino broke the silence with a plea, "I lost a very valuable piece of equipment when I had to cut off the main chute Jane. I saw it fall, its pink in color and it can't be far away. Help me look for it."

They peeled off their jump gear and began to search the area when all of a sudden Jane sank down into the mud on her knees in utter thankfulness. She was overwhelmed with the thought that God had just saved their lives. That holy understanding had her face down on the dirty field overcome with emotion of how very different it could have turned out.

Ino called out to her from the other side of the mud splattered ground shouting, "Jane...Jane did you find it?" When there was no response he sensed something was wrong and came running back to where she was finding her absolutely covered in mud.

Jane looked up at him, with tears streaming down her mud caked face, creating little rivulets of joy, and smiled.

Ino understood and offered his hand to give her a pull-up and noticed in the distance the Jeep heading in their direction.

"Look, Jane, here comes our ride."

When the Jeep pulled up, the driver Ben said, "Boy this jump will go down in the annals of history of 'Free Falls.' We should celebrate with a toast!"

As they made their way back to the hangar, Jane had only one thought in mind... *"To God be the glory."*

172

Epilogue

"Jane? Jane?" called Chris in a low tone as he gently shook her shoulder, "Jane, wake up."

The storms of the night before had lulled her to sleep in the chair perched in front of the doors that led to the small balcony in their apartment. She still had the picture of herself as a little girl clutched in her hand when Chris woke her.

"Oh Chris…" she stammered, slowly becoming aware of her surroundings. "The storm woke me up and I couldn't get back to sleep," she murmured. "My, oh my…I started looking at a few pictures and when I dozed off, I mean it was so very real to me, just as it all happened. They were all there with me again. Papa and Mama, Karl, Nocki, Avi, Gretchen, and even the little frogs Max and Mortiz," Jane insisted. Her eyes and mind slowly starting to clear from her night in the chair as she continued, "It was like a movie, the best movie ever. All of it came to me, so many memories that I am simply overwhelmed."

Chris, steady as usual, said nothing but his face spoke for him, steel blue eyes understanding that his wife of forty-eight years had a far different night's sleep because he slept right through the storms. He put a hand on her shoulder in support.

Jane looked at Chris directly and said, "So many, many times I could have died in a bombing like many of my friends and neighbors did, but I was spared. MS has pushed me to my knees time and time again and yet I have still found the strength to stand up after each setback. I have had to say goodbye to those I love and those who have loved me, and yet I remain. I never thought I would find love again and then you came into my life and accepted me just as I am, and we have built a wonderful life together."

Tears were rolling down her face as she spoke.

She looked down at the picture she held in her trembling hand, then she looked at the photographs of her parents and brothers, her son Eddie, and Chris in his flight suit all strewn about on the table next to the chair. There was the photo of the Angel of Peace in all its glory and the picture of her flying above the earth after she jumped out of an airplane at 10,000 feet.

She let all of the memories, images and emotions wash over her.

"Since I was a little girl, the Lord has kept me, guided me, healed me, and loved me no matter how far down I have fallen, no matter how scared I was," she said quietly. "He has always lifted me when I didn't think I could take another step, he showed me the way. I think the reason I had all those dreams last night was a gift, a reminder from God."

"What was the reminder?" Chris asked.

Jane cleared her throat, stood up from the chair and looked into the morning sun, closed her eyes and said in strong voice, *"...Philippians 4:13... I can do all things through Christ who strengthens me."*

Then she turned her gaze back to Chris, smiled broadly and with a twinkle in her eye said,

"My life has *been a matter of grace..."*

Made in the USA
Middletown, DE
11 October 2020